by Mina Loy

Lunar Baedeker (1923)
Lunar Baedeker & Time-Tables (1958)
At the Door of the House (1980)
Love Songs (1981)
Virgins Plus Curtains (1981)
The Last Lunar Baedeker (1982)
Insel (1991)

INSEL

MINA LOY

EDITED BY
ELIZABETH ARNOLD

BLACK SPARROW PRESS
SANTA ROSA 1991

ACKNOWLEDGMENTS

I wish to thank Mina Loy's daughter, Joella Bayer, for her encouragement and support. Thanks also goes to Loy's literary executor, Roger L. Conover, and the Beinecke Rare Book and Manuscript Library at Yale University for permission to publish *Insel*. Keith Tuma suggested changes in the afterword, and without Robert von Hallberg's early support of my interest in Loy, this book may never have appeared in print. Helen Bryan's fluency in German eased my way through books and articles about Richard Oelze. Finally, I offer my thanks to Jack, for his patience and his sharp eye, and for his love. E.A.

LIBRARY OF CONGRESS CATALOGING-IN-PUBLICATION DATA

Loy, Mina, 1882-1966
   Insel / Mina Loy ; edited by Elizabeth Arnold.
      p.   cm.
   ISBN 0-87685-854-X (cloth) : — ISBN 0-87685-855-8 (deluxe cloth) : — ISBN 0-87685-853-1 (pbk.) :
   I. Arnold, Elizabeth, 1958-   II. Title.
PS3523.O975I57   1991
813'.52—dc20
                             91-29061
                              CIP

TABLE OF CONTENTS

Editor's Note

THE **BASE TEXT** for this edition of *Insel* is a type-script manuscript labeled "Third draft, copy 1" at the Beinecke Rare Book and Manuscript Library at Yale University. This manuscript was prepared and corrected by Mina Loy. Her footnotes have been incorporated into Appendix A, which gives English translations of all foreign phrases except those which are clearly translated in the text of the novel. Where Loy indicated section breaks by triple spacing, we have numbered each section. A few minor corrections of punctuation and typing errors have been made, and foreign words and phrases have been italicized. In general, however, Loy's idiosyncrasies have been preserved. Throughout the manuscript, Loy used British and American spellings interchangeably. For the purposes of this edition, we have used all American spellings, following the ninth edition of *Webster's Collegiate Dictionary*.

FOREWORD

INSEL, ORIGINALLY CONCEIVED as part of a larger narrative called *Islands in the Air,* is one of a number of fugitive prose works written by Mina Loy more than a half-century ago. It is also the most substantial of these virtually unknown texts and the first to be published. As autobiographical as it is fictional, and as grounded in psychological truth as in hallucinatory transformation, the non-romance is being presented here as, for lack of a better term, a *roman à clef.* And while it is true that Man Ray, Salvador Dali, Arthur Cravan, Julien Levy and Joseph Cornell peep in and out of the narrative, *Insel* is orthogonal to established genres. Compositionally, this is another of Mina Loy's self-induced, *sui generis* hybrids—a display of legerdemain by the poet and legendarian whom Arthur Cravan called the "greatest psychologist who has ever lived."

Mina Loy would be the last to call herself a novelist, or to answer, for that matter, to any of the names which refer to producers of the things she made—plays, poems, hats, manifestoes, paintings, collages, essays, sculptures, inventions, crafts,

‖ 9

fashions, lampshades, drapes, designs, dresses. She wrote, she painted, she made things. She did so with a self-possessed certainty, oblivious to the notion of audience and unconcerned about what impact these activities might have on the building of a reputation, or a career: "I leave that to my post-mortem examination."

The business card she used in the 1930s gave no indication of literary interests; it simply listed the types of lamps, lampshades and illuminating devices she confected out of spare parts and implausible materials in a small shop in Paris until her patience with business—and with her partner, Peggy Guggenheim—ran out. Verbal and visual creation were at the center of her life, but the exigencies of raising a family and making a living made writing and painting, by definition, something she did on the side. Yet if in her lifetime, conditions scarcely favored an artist who gave proof of her talent in every direction but declined to take herself seriously in any of them, the guilty conscience of our age provides the conditions for corrective examination.

The fact is, Mina Loy, the personality, was terribly complex, and, so far as the "artist" is concerned, completely self-invented. The enigma she presents yields itself more easily to entertaining anecdotes than critical perspectives. She moved as freely in the literary and artistic avant-garde circles of Florence and Montparnasse in the 1910s and '20s as she did among the lost souls and fallen angels of the Bowery in the 1940s and '50s. She was a living reproach to the idea of the canonical, refusing to meet the art world on its terms, and brushing off the institutions and individuals who could "make" her. What other poet, then or now, would dare compare T. S. Eliot's translations of Valéry to the experience of "falling down a vegetarian's lavatory"?

Mina Loy bandaged soldiers and took in the homeless. There is nothing wrong with an artist forsaking her art to prevent the injured from becoming invalids or the starving from becoming hopeless, but it is not as metaphorically rich, or as symbolically elegant, as forsaking it to play chess, or to take up boxing. So what if Ezra Pound, William Carlos Williams and Yvor Winters believed she was one of the two or three most promising poets of her age, or if Robert McAlmon, Margaret Anderson and Alfred Kreymborg published her with as much conviction as they did Ernest Hemingway, Wallace Stevens and Marianne Moore? She could not have cared less what anyone thought when her first, strange poems appeared in the pages of little Greenwich Village magazines, causing a flurry of polemic for and against. She shunned acceptance as much as rejection, and looked elsewhere—to numerology, Christian Science and theories of facial destiny—for her canonicals. Mina Loy was a woman whose company Djuna Barnes, Natalie Barney and Mabel Dodge preferred; but they could never have enough of her, because she was always elusive, occupied or on the move. She distrusted equally attention and neglect, whether of the male or female variety. Except in one relationship, with a man who gave her enough of both in a few short months to last her a lifetime, and whose love of elusion and belief in Elysium was absolute—Fabian Lloyd, a.k.a. Arthur Cravan, the poet-boxer-missing person whom she refers to as "Colossus" in *Insel.*

Ten years ago, in the introduction to the Jargon Society's edition of *The Last Lunar Baedeker,* the volume of Mina Loy's "nearly complete" poems assembled for the centennial of her birth, I tried to make a case for Mina Loy as a "difficult," and therefore "neglected," poet. Today, partly because of the cult of reverse-chic which has attached itself to Jargon publications, and partly because of the desire on the part of certain critical establishments to "claim" her, it has become fashionable to introduce newcomers to her work with a justifying recommendation—Neglected Woman Poet—as if lack of awareness on the part of a wider public compliments the perspicacity of the discoverer, the one who is being invited, as if by password, to come inside. The tendency to legendize, rather than legitimize, Mina Loy's career is understandable, given certain proclivities of her own. But it also puts the work at risk of being marginalized again.

Hardly a month goes by anymore without an editor requesting permission to include her work in a forthcoming anthology, or a graduate student of English literature or art history inquiring about some aspect of her life or work. Her biography has been commissioned by Farrar, Straus & Giroux, her poems have begun appearing in translation, and, as I write, her likeness of Man Ray and his of her hang in the National Portrait Gallery. An exhibition of her art work is being considered, a film is being discussed, and another edition of her collected poems is being prepared. Mina Loy is no longer the missing modernist, waiting to be discovered, but a poet whose reputation and readership are very much on the rise. The publication of this book, unthinkable ten years ago, is but one more example of the rightful rehabilitation of her name from obscurity.

Excerpts from and extensive references to *Insel* first appeared in Germany in 1989, when Renate Damsch-Wiehager's important monograph on the German painter Richard Oelze (*Richard Oelze: Ein alter Meister der Moderne*) was published in Munich. Oelze, on whom the character Insel is based, was a misanthropic surrealist who lived in Paris from 1933 to 1936. At the time, Mina Loy was standing in the thick of surrealist traffic. As the mother-in-law and sole Paris agent for Julien Levy, she had helped to organize the first exhibition of surrealist art in America at the Julien Levy Gallery in New York in 1932. Although Mina Loy considered Oelze a "congenital surrealist," temperamentally he was more of an anti-surrealist surrealist, an artist out of place in their midst, and one whose inspiration came from outside Surrealism's main currents. He refused to enter into easy consanguinity with his "fellow" surrealists, who were known for their group dynamics and collaborative projects. He was an outsider; he stood apart.

But with Mina Loy he developed a strange intimacy; if *Insel* is an accurate portrait of their relationship, she valued "the lovely equilibrium his companionship conveyed to me," but more than that, she sensed he carried some essential mystery, and felt her psyche engage his with "a premonition of some treasure" to which she responded as to a "cosmic imperative." In *Insel*, initially, the narrator sets out to write Insel's biography, but soon abandons the idea in favor of the more absorbing compulsion to understand the "radial starfish under-pattern of his life." This becomes her obsession, but also her disease, as she comes to realize that his pathetically dependent "self" needs a witness to exist, that he is disembodied except when he is able to invade "the furnished mind of a spectator." He suffers, it seems, "from the incredible handicap of only being able to *mature* in the imagination of another." While Mina Loy recognized that she was probably "the collaborative audience to his finest act," she also realized that by hostaging her imagination to his, she risked sinking into the abyss of autism in which she found him, making herself the victim rather than the agent of her own creative power. Her ultimate act of compassion—release—is directed toward herself.

In 1961, with the help of an agent, Mina Loy offered *Insel* to one of America's most distinguished literary presses with the hope of getting it published before she died. The publisher declined. Despite his fascination with the work, he questioned whether it was really a novel, and thought it still needed a lot of work. Mina Loy was 79 at the time, and incapable, he supposed, of revising it herself. Who could help her, he wondered. Thirty years went by, and no one tried. Then Elizabeth Arnold, a graduate student at the University of Chicago, encountered *Insel* at the Beinecke Library at Yale in the course of doing research for her thesis on Mina Loy. She liked what she read, and to her credit she understood that nothing had to be altered. She is the book's editor, and we have her to thank for bringing this island into the air.

As for the rest, Mina Loy said it best in describing how she felt upon finishing *Insel*: "I feel there's something wrong—& at the same time something right—I can't see it yet from the other side."

Roger L. Conover
June 27, 1991
Portland, Maine

INSEL

1

THE FIRST I HEARD of Insel was the story of a madman, a more or less surrealist painter, who, although he had nothing to eat, was hoping to sell a picture to buy a set of false teeth. He wanted, he said, to go to the bordel but feared to disgust a prostitute with a mouthful of roots. The first I saw of this pathetically maimed celebrity were the tiny fireworks he let off in his eyes when offered a ham sandwich. What an incongruous end, my subconscious idly took note, for a man who must once have had such phenomenal attraction for women. And he wants them of the consistency of motor tires . . . my impression faded off. For, to my workaday consciousness, he only looked like an embryonic mind locked in a dilapidated structure. I heard plenty of talk about his pictures, but I was afraid to visit his studio as, to all accounts, his lunacy rendered him unsafe. It rather took me aback, when a few days after his casual introduction to me, he paid me a call. I had been giving tea to my little model after the pose when he arrived. Her Slavonic person was colored a lovely luminous yellow, owing to some liver complaint, and her sturdy legs, which *I supposed he could not see* for she was already dressed for the street, were of such substance as sun-warmed stone. With the promptness of a magnet picking up a pin, he made a date with her for the following day.

Facing each other they possessed voluptuous attributes the poor will find in one another unmarred by an unwholesomeness which is mutual. The model, tremendously engaged in hoping to have a baby to persuade her lover to make her his wife, later decided it would not be politic to turn up. Not without regret, however, for "I *like* him," she confided to me, squeezing her hands together in delight.

As for myself, he cleared my recollections of the prejudice for his madness as he sat disseminating in my amusing sitting room a pleasant neutrality, pulling one's sympathies in his direction. And as the afternoon wore out, it was as if a dove had flown through the window and settled upon a chair. Whenever his features obtruded on the sight some impulse of the mind would push them out of the way as if one obeyed an implicit appeal not to look at him but rather give in to the mischievous peace which seemed to enclose him in a sheath.

That evening I began a letter to a friend: "Aaron's latest surrealist is absolutely divine. He has painted a picture that's not so very hot in any particular detail—a gigantic back of a commonplace woman looking at the sky. It's here to be shipped with the consignment I am sending to Aaron, and

I swear whenever I'm in the room with it I catch myself staring at that sky waiting, oblivious of time, for whatever is about to appear in it. Most eerie! The man himself is just like that. He did not say anything in particular, but you felt you were in the room with an invisible will-o'-the-wisp, and that any moment it might light up. He's the son, he said, of tiny working people and seems the most delicate and refined soul I've ever come across. He has an evening suit, but never an occasion to wear it, so he puts it on when he paints his pictures, first having meticulously cleaned everything in his studio. Now, I don't mean he's a delicate soul because he paints in evening dress—! That's just one of his stories I remember. I shall probably find this quality exists only in my imagination because there's something fundamentally black-magicky about the surrealists, and I feel that going in that direction, his face, that looks almost luminous from starvation, will turn out to be a death's head after all.

"It's funny how people who get mixed up with black magic do suddenly look like death's heads— they will grin and there is nothing but a skull peering at you, at once it's all over—but you remember. Sex is an exception. He is permanently a skull with ligaments attached, having the false eyes of an angel, and, at the back of them his cranium full of intellectual dust. Often they look like goat's. While Moto has the expression of an outrageous ram, his wife the re-animated mummy of an Egyptian sorceress. In fact, they are very, in their fantastic ways, expressive of their art, which after all takes on such shapes as would seethe from a cauldron overcast by some wizard's tortuous will."

The letter was never finished, for, and this was often to be the case, once he had left, his person would gradually gather together till at last one could normally *see* him as he really was, or had been when present. Tall, his torso concave, he was so emaciated that from his waist down he looked like a stork on one leg. His queer ashen face seemed veritably patched with the bruises of some physical defeat that had left him pretty repulsive. One's mind, released from the unaccountable influence of his nature's emanations, readjusted the time spent in his company to the rational proportion of an interview with a plain, eccentric, somewhat threadbare man, strangely pitiable in a premature old age. His manner alone remained unchanged by this surprising reverse—it was of an extreme distinction. Owing to this, before my letter drew to a close, I had lost the impression of whatever had inspired it, finding myself very much in the situation of Titania confronted with entirely meaningless donkey's ears.

It argued a certain good fortune, in Insel's timing of his next visit, that it should coincide with that of a German girl, as his absolute inability to acquire any language to add to his own must have made his inhabitation of a foreign land a somewhat lonely affair. But in how far I found it at last impossible to determine, so narrowly his unformulated existence seemed associated with itself. Her visit was fortunate for me also, for later on, in our checking up on the subject of this very Insel, she, so common-sensed and unimaginative, was able to clear my doubt as to whether it was I who must be mentally deranged. Wishing to get on familiar terms with an acknowledged surrealist, we took him to a cafe, and, in the embracing glare of a locality above all others conducive to the liberal exchange of confidences between the most heterogeneous people, the meager personality of this stranded German opened up.

I still retain wisps of the irreal crises in his footloose career that, as he related it, grew up, story by story, a frail edifice of lies and memory out of our marble tabletop. It was securely buttressed by groups of obese tradesmen who, in their agglomerated leisure, were playing *belote*. He told us, his gray eyes atwinkle with the inner security the possession of a strange surplus fortune, balancing destitution, gives to men of genius, he had solved the problem of keeping alive without any money and thus had lived for sixteen years.

A man who finds himself economically nude, should logically, in the thickset iron forest of our industrial structure, be banged to death from running into its fearfully rigid supports. He is again the primordial soft-machine without the protective overall of the daily job in which his fellows wend their way to some extent unbattered by this sphere of activity. For them, the atrocious jaws of the gigantic organism will open at fixed intervals and spit at them rations sufficient to sustain their coalescence with the screeching, booming, crashing dynamism of the universal "works." For the *révolté*, for one incapable of taking it as it is, this metal forest of coin bearing machinery will partially revert to the condition of nature preserved in him, and show patches of moss as if he had projected there some of the verdure rooted in him. Oases of leisure, succorable, soft if ragged lining to the cage of practical mankind, these mossy refuges, along the life of a wayward spirit who refuses to do as he is told, preferring to find out for himself what to do, mostly materialize as the hospitalities of modest little women who find a temporary relief from their innate anxiety in association with an irresponsible man in whom the honest desire for survival of his creative impulse gets dishonestly mixed up with his amatory instinct.

Insel, as he talked, seemed to be recurrently emerging from predicaments of which, if some were lamentable, many were quite diaphanous as though nothing of him but the most subtle aspects of his peculiar temperament had got into them— He varnished his painting of the past with a gentle irritation of commentarial laughter. Unlike other men, he took delight in confessing that all his women had deserted him, divorced him, thrown him out. How he had pled with those women to have patience. "I am tired of supporting a waster," they would tell him at last. "But they were wrong," averred Insel. "While I appeared irretrievably idle, *Ich habe mich entwickelt*—I was developing," he explained, the mischief dancing defiantly in his eyes. And this *Entwicklung* I would not estimate blurred my view of Insel. I saw his image grown suddenly faint, imploring the shadow of woman "—to only wait—in the end—the end—I shall achieve glory."

These unfortunate separations, throwing him back upon the desert base from which he was ever setting out anew, formed part of the frieze of disaster through which he represented himself as forever fleeing under the vicious darts of his drastic horoscope.

Housing his poverty as animals tracked down enter abandoned holes or a honeyless bee might return to an empty hive—of all the makeshift burrows he found for himself in an unearned earth, so desolate and perilous seemed his escapade in some far away, dismantled villa he described to us that it has stuck in my mind. He had lived there one summer, with some caressive *Mädchen* who, when she left the place, had forgotten to ask him to give up his key. And so it was that Insel, fallen once more under the heel of fate, crept back to that love-swept lair and, shutting himself up in one of the rooms, lived on the floor. "I could draw there," he pointed out to us thankfully. And one saw him, day alone, morrow alone, where the air was the breath of his own hunger, warily sneaking out at dark in search of a remnant of food, or, just as possibly, so complex is the status of the artist, dining with affable millionaires every other night. It comes back to me now that Insel had started this episode as the story of a haunted house.

"One day when I had hidden there so long," he said, "as to make one with the everlasting silence, I was startled by the sound of footfalls descending the stairs. 'Who could descend having never ascended?' I asked myself. 'What could have embodied itself under the roof to come down upon my isolation?' I at once turned the key in my lock and waited, listening to those fearful feet. At intervals they would halt, and at every halt I could hear the echoes of heavy fists pounding on a door. And the footsteps grew louder, the pounding nearer—to the pounding of my heart." Frau Feirlein and I hung on his words while, "Those heavy unreal fists fell in a rain of blows on the last door—the door," continued Insel, "that shut off the bearable emptiness of the room I was living in from the unbearable emptiness of the house as a whole."

I imagined his quivering breast receiving, through the transmission of his fear, the ghostly blows aimed at the door affording his outer defense as he stood face to face with it. "Not daring to stir," he proceeded, "I was almost choking for terror it would hear me breathe, when gradually I perceived a softer noise come to succeed that ominous pounding. I do not know what impulse this aroused in me, my one desire having been to remain undiscovered, that caused me so suddenly to fling myself on that door and to open it—outside stood a very severe looking *Huissier*. He was sealing up the rooms. And, as usual," added Insel in utter discouragement, "*They* hauled me before a magistrate."

His father, he said, was a *Schlosser,* which turned out to mean "blacksmith," and very early in Insel's life, as in the episode in the empty villa, his destiny appeared to me to get mixed up with keys. I cannot remember in detail the vague accidents in which his minor salvations depended upon keys except for a fleeting impression of Insel crawling under his destitute couch in search of some kind of key to a gas meter confused with an intermittent flitting in and out of gas men and electricity bill collectors who would come to cut him off and who, owing to some either mental or manual hocus-pocus of Insel with the key, ended by turning the gas or electricity on. Thus leaving him at least two elements of life.

"Don't *Schlossers* make keys?" I asked.

"Surely," he agreed.

"Well, you've *inherited* the keys your father made. You'll see the whole of your life will turn on a key. Some people are accompanied throughout their career by a fixation of their destiny—yours is a key. While Dali, for instance, is fated to the most extravagant of publicities. He is inclined to accept my theory, for some of the shrillest gags in his already fabulous advertisement were the result of sheer coincidence, yet pointing out plainly the effective procedure to be followed thenceforth. He told me it all originated with his first lecture on surrealism in Spain, when the mayor, who was acting as chairman, fell down dead at his feet, almost as soon as he began—a windfall for journalists."

Insel, as if after this he feared his trips along the road to ruin might fall a little flat, changing his tempo, began to show off, surprising us with a burst of magnificence, he became so hilariously wealthy he juggled a fortune. "I spent ten millions in a year," he enthused. "Not one car, but bunches of cars I gave each of my friends, and the orchestras I ordered, the clusters of beautiful women I hung upon myself in those Berlin nights."

"Where did you get it all?"

"Forging," he replied, with the same elation with which he had dispensed for our entertainment his retrospective largess. "*Es war wirklich prachtvoll—*we made bank notes in sheaves. You see, as a boy I was apprentice lithographer, and my technique was so remarkable I got raked in by a gang of crooks. We practically bought up Berlin before we were caught, and I was only in jail nine months."

"How was that?"

"Oh, one of the gang who escaped arrest used his influence. But I had time to reflect," he commented. "I saw other careers open to talent. In that long solitude I conceived of a greater wealth than the wealth of banks. Within myself I found the artist."

2

ON THE GROUNDS THAT he was starving to
death, he would exact from us the minutiae of
advice on his alimentary problems to subsequent-
ly toss all advice aside in his audacious irrespon-
sibility. Presenting himself as a pauper to the
charitable organization of the Quakers, he had
harvested, among other things, packages of maca-
roni and several pounds of cocoa, and as if these
staple aliments were already consumed, he
begged us to counsel him what to do now. He shook
his head over the suggestion that he go there again.
"My last supply is yet too recent," he objected. But,
Frau Feirlein told me, on the morrow he presented
himself at her flat with these same Quaker gifts intact as an offering preliminary to his indistinct court-
ship. "What is the use of cocoa to me," he argued
with my bewilderment, "I have no sugar." And, for
some vague reason, one took the opposition of his
prodigality to his mendicancy as a matter of course.
This reason consisted in an intuition, so deeply im-
bedded in one's subconscious it would not rise to the
surface of the mind until the final phase in one's
analysis of him—that this skeletal symbol of an

ultimate starvation had need of a food we knew not of. Throughout his angling for compassion on behalf of his utter destitution, one never resented his open carelessness in throwing back the fish.

Meanwhile, his reserved distinction, as of an aristocrat who should in a lasting revolution have experienced yet unimaginably survived the guillotine, was so consistent it claimed one's respect for his nonsensical manner of being alive. But once was this impression dispelled when, in courteous haste to answer a question, he shifted the part of a hard roll sandwich he was eating, out of the way, horrifyingly developing a Dali-like protuberance of elongated flesh with his flaccid facial tissue. As if unexpectedly the *Schlosser* one had hitherto been incapable of relating to him had at length intruded upon us with his anvil stuffed in his cheek.

Only towards the close of his reminiscences did he seem to have shared a responsibility with normal men: "They sent me to war," he told us wryly, voicing that unconvincing complaint against their perpetual situation in the ridiculous made by people who, pleasing to laugh at themselves, one suspects of aiding destiny in detaining them there, "in two left-foot boots, and," trotting his fingers along the table in a swerve, "the one *would* follow the other," he explained as the mental eye also followed that earlier Insel—out of the ranks; on the march to a war that, at its blasting zenith, ceased to be war, for, in elaborating his martial adventures,

Insel turned out to have been taking part in a film.

A wound up automaton running down, Insel ceased among the clatter of our amusement.

"I know how you can make money," I exclaimed agog with enthusiasm. "Write your biography."

"I am a painter," he objected. "It would take too long building a style."

"You'd only have to write the way you paint. Minutely, meticulously—like an ant! Can you remember every moment, every least incident of your life?"

"All," he replied decisively.

"Then start at once."

"It would need so much careful editing. In the raw it would be scandalous—"

"Scandalous," I cried scandalized—"the truth? Anyway you can write under a pseudonym."

"People would recognize me."

"Don't you know anything of the world? The artist's vindication does not lie in 'what happens to him' but in what shape he comes out."

"Oh," said Insel disinhibiting, "very well. It's not the material that is wanting," he sighed wearily, "the *stacks* of manuscript notes I have accumulated!"

Then, "No," he reversed, "it's not my medium."

"Insel," I asked breathlessly, "would you let *me* write it?"

"That would be feasible," he answered

interested. "We will make a pact. Get me to America and you *have* the biography."

"Done," I decided. "I'll write at once. America shall clamor for you."

"Don't overdo it," warned Insel, "it never works."

"You can have your dinners with me and tell me— Can you really remember—the minutest details?"

"Every one," he assured me.

"What a book," I sighed with satisfaction.

"Flight from Doom—every incident distorted to the pattern of an absurd destiny," Insel was looking delighted with himself.

He came out to dinner on a few evenings and I would talk with him for hours. The minute details were fewer than I had bargained for, his leitmotif being his strangeness in so seldom having spoken.

"My parents noticed it at once," he told me. "As a child I would remain absolutely silent for six months at a time."

He did not give a fig for heredity. All his relatives were chatty.

Another thing he had found in himself was his aptitude for housework. He had once married a stenographer, who simply *could* not arrange the kitchen with the same precision as he.

"She tried so hard—for so long. She never came up to the mark. What I disliked was her plagiarism. Why," demanded Insel with retrospective annoyance, "could she not have worked out a system of her own?"

So they separated. Later, when Insel and I became uncannily intimate I understood what his unique orderliness had done to the girl—given her the jitters!

Nevertheless, he himself seemed sometimes to have difficulty in locating things. Once during coffee he drifted off to the lavabo and on his return took a seat some tables away from the one at which he had left me. In the same slightly deferent sociable concern he continued to "pay attention"—

The strain on this biography would consist in his too facile superposing of separate time—his reminiscences flitted about from one end of his life to the other.

"I saw an antique dealer carrying a picture to a taxi the other day—a portrait of some women. They were extraordinarily attractive to me; I was sure we would have been profoundly congenial. It was labeled 'The Brontë Sisters.' Do you know of anyone by that name?" asked Insel, who had not read Goethe nor heard of Shakespeare. "The dealer told me they were authoresses—I feel I should care for what they have written."

"The sister Emily wrote *Wuthering Heights*. I suppose it is one of the greatest novels ever written. I never remember for very long, after having read it, what it's about—yet whenever I think of it—I find myself standing on wild moors—alone with the elements—elements become articulate—. *You* would care for it very much."

I began to think it improbable I should even find

a basis for this biography. He was so at variance with himself, he existed on either side of a paradox. Even as he begged for food to throw away, forever in search of a haven, he preferred *any* discomfort to going home. Constantly he thanked his stars for an iron constitution—while obviously in an alarming state of health.

3

AT LAST THE BIOGRAPHY aborted as had the Quaker oats.

The first stage of Insel's intimacy completed, when he evidently intended to let you further "in on" his show, he insisted on your reading Kafka, just as on assisting at a foreign opera one is handed a book of the words.

Study this well he tacitly commended. It will give you an angle of approach. "In Kafka," he explained, "I found a foreshadowing of my hounded existence, recognized the relentless drive of my peculiar misfortune."

Der Prozess was the volume he borrowed to lend me, and I lay awake reading on and on and on, curious for the book to begin, when, with one eye still open, I came upon the end to fall asleep in the unsatisfied certainty of having become acquainted with an undeniable, yet perhaps the most useless, genius who ever lived.

Enraged with bitter disappointment, *"Zum Teufel,"* I berated Insel, when he appeared for our next session. If he was a lunatic, he was prodigious, dressing up his insanity in another man's madness. It was no use to me. Flight from Doom, with its pattern of absurd destiny, had already been written.

"You atrocious fake—you have no life to write—you're *acting* Kafka!"

"And I," answered Insel, as I turned him out, "see clearly into *you*. Your brain is all Brontë." Flying the colors of his victory, he sauntered off.

4

I THOUGHT I HAD dropped Insel. I was mistaken. Some weeks later I was writing letters when all of a sudden I stopped. An urgent telepathy impinging on my mind, I automatically dashed off a card. When I looked to see what I had so unpreparedly written—this is how it began:

Insel:

In a hole? If it's of use,
can advance you what
you are getting from
the .... Gallery.

"It is interesting," Insel was to remark significant-
ly later on. "Your note to me was couched in
flawless German."

For a while I sat wondering to *what* appeal, and
why, I had answered. *I did not care* if Insel were in
trouble. Obviously he fabricated trouble and far be
it from me to deprive him of it—. I threw the card into
the waste paper basket, and started for the post.
When I had opened the front door I shut it again and
retrieved the postcard. Before the letter-box I put it
in my pocket and turned away, only to go back—
with a relieved determination I posted it.

Insel must have crossed my message for in a
couple of hours he panted into my place all
undone, despairingly waving a sheet of blue
paper.

"*Das blaue Papier,*" he articulated hoarsely,
ducking his head as if the *Papier* was one of a
shower of such sheets bombarding him in his dash
for escape.

"Something the matter? Have a *porto.* Sit on a chair. Whatever it is—out with it!"

"*Das blaue Papier,*" he reiterated, casting a haunted look over his shoulder. On its return that look fell in with some photographs of paintings lying on the table.

"*Whose* pictures are these?" asked Insel, immediately collected, and staring at each in turn with entire attention."*Who* could have done these?"

"They are mine."

"You are an extraordinarily gifted woman," he said, still staring at them. "Oh, how I wish I could read your book."

"It's not like those pictures," I laughed and told him their brief history.

" 'Those' are my 'last exhibition' cancelled the moment the dealer set eyes on them."

"Good God," muttered Insel under his breath.

"I felt, if I were to go back, begin a universe all over again, forget all form I am familiar with, evoking a chaos from which I could draw forth incipient form, that at last the female brain might achieve an act of creation."

I did not know this as yet, but the man seated before me holding a photo in his somewhat invalid hand had done this very thing—visualized the mists of chaos curdling into shape. But with a male difference.

Well, it turned out that the blue paper was a summons for rent involving the evacuation of his studio.

Insel's system in such emergency was this:

Never to pay. To work himself into an individualistic kind of epilepsy whenever served with a summons or notified to appear in court to explain why the money was not forthcoming. Computing illusory accounts to find the exact sum he could promise to pay by a certain date, knowing full well he would not be able to pay anything at all, in order to scare himself into fits awaiting the fatal appointment.

Now one could watch him following the path of pursuit at an easy canter, having proved he had something definite to flee from.

His role was helplessness personified. So here he was without a roof. In spite of the ceiling a pitiless rain seemed to be falling upon him already.

Whenever I have seen poor people asleep on stone seats in the snow, like complementary colors in the eyes, there arise in my mind unused ballrooms and vacationers' apartments whose central heating warms a swarming absence. To the pure logician this association of ideas might suggest a possible trans-occupation of cubic space, while mere experience will prove that the least of being alive is transacted in space, so much does sheer individuality exceed it; that providing a refuge for a single castaway brings results more catastrophic than a state of siege.

So I kept saying to myself, "Remember, you don't care a damn what happens to this thin man." While what he did was to fill the room with all men who are over-lean. And the room fell open, extending to space—as such—to remind me of my futile superposition of stone benches on ballrooms. My lips opened automatically. "Don't be fools," I admonished them. "Keep out of this. You'll get me into an unnecessary jam." In the end I must have given in, for I heard myself telling him, to my despair, he could live in my flat when I had gone to the country. "If that's any help," I added dubiously. "It solves half my problem," he thanked me with appreciative warmth.

The result of this lapse of protective selfishness was days of agony. I had intended to run off to the country at once. But now—I sat looking at that apartment obsessed with the necessity of disencumbering it of personalia. The onus of trying to make up one's mind where to begin overpowered me.

The psychic effort of retracting oneself from the creative dimension where one can remain indefinitely—like a conscious rock—immovable—in intellectual transmutation of long since absorbed actualities, while the present actuality is let to go hang—was devastating.

The contemplation of a bureau whose drawers must be emptied—the idea of some sort of classification of manuscript notes and miscellaneous papers— that in habitual jumble are easily selectable by the remembrance of their subconscious "arrangement," the effort to concentrate on something in which one takes no interest, which is the major degradation of women, gives pain so acute that, in magnifying a plausible task to an inextricable infinity of deadly detail, the mind disintegrates. The only thing to do is to rush out of the house and forget it all. So disliking to leave one's work in favor of some practical imperative, in begrudging the time to undertake, one wastes triple the time in being averse to thinking.

Something would have to be done about it. Fortunately, after more than a week of this paralyzing resistance, I came across a long painting overall. Its amplitude made something click in my brain. I at once became animated with that operative frenzy which succeeds to such periods of unproductive strain. Sewing up its neck and sleeves on the Singer, I obtained a corpse-like sack, and stuffing it full of scribbles I tied it up, and, throwing it into a superfluous room, locked the door on it with a sigh of relief. I was once more myself.

In the meanwhile Insel had come to take me to see one of his rare paintings in the possession of a friend who was liable to feed him at crucial moments.

In the taxi I inquired, "*Was haben Sie schönes erlebt* since I saw you?"

"I had two negresses at once," he answered, all aglitter.

"Two," I echoed anxiously. "I hope you didn't have to pay them."

"Oh, no," he assured me.

"So they liked the look of you," I teased with friendly disdain.

40 ‖

"Yes," he concurred apologetically.

"And—was it nice?"

"Well," he reflected, "I thought it was going to be nice. And now the trouble is to get rid of them. And what have you *erlebt?*" he commented.

"Not quite so *much*—anyhow."

I saw the picture. Its various forms, at once embryonic and precocious, being half-evolved and of degenerate purpose, were overgrown with a hair that never grew anywhere else—it was so fine. And when our host had gone out of the room Insel stared at it amazed. His face became rigid with incredulity. "I cannot believe I ever painted anything so wonderful," he murmured. "How did I do it?" he begged himself to explain.

When we got out on the street again I walked some paces off parallel to him in order to observe him. Adverse remarks with ordinary men it is politic to keep to oneself, while to withhold one's comments from Insel would have appeared impolite. His very personality taking the form of a question mark, it would have shown a lack of perspicacity when intentionally confronted with a self-composed conundrum, not to attempt unobserved, the intriguer, underrated.

Curiosity he constrained to stand off to take his measure, mentality, to pivot him for noting whether there were any creases in his aural suit. As those who are of the body, whom other bodies have traffic with, slap each other on the back, with Insel intercourse depended on putting out feelers among the loose matter of psychologic nebulae.

"You walk so weirdly," I said. "Are you one of those surrealists who have taken up black magic?"

Totally bewildered, he exclaimed, "Whatever is that?" Yet, like all who have to do with any form of magic, he apparently had lost some of his specific gravity.

He was passing over the light-reflecting pavement in his shabby black as if a rigid crow, although with folded wings should skim.

"Acra," I said, "sends dreams across the Atlantic."

"He could not," protested Insel, off his guard. "He has not got the *power*."

There is a way of speaking that word peculiar to those alone who have wielded it—that way was his.

And he glided on, turning towards me his face hung with deflated muscles one felt could be blown about by the wind.

"You cannot glide," it defied me, and I noticed how I was keeping my distance in my effort to "get at him."

He had for the moment the stick-fast aloofness of an evil presentiment—the air of a priest of some criminal cult. All the same, this slight impression of criminality he gave off at intervals I did not receive as a direct impress on my own mind, but as a glimpse of a conviction he hid within himself.

"Aren't you rather bad?" I laughingly inquired.

"Everybody imagines I am the devil, and," he

answered forlornly shrugging his shoulders, "there's no harm in me at all."

When we fell into line once more, he resumed the uniformity of all people making for a cafe.

I finally gave Insel the key. His mimicry of salvation convinced me my distress, after all, had not been in vain.

But, oh horror! On arriving at the country, I suddenly *seemed* to remember the charwoman pouring some Normanol from an antique bottle I had told her to clean into an empty gin bottle. Normanol, being a dissolvent for rhodoid very much stronger than cutex which dissolves the cuticle around the fingernails, I had a shocking vision of Insel's diaphanous intestines entirely disappearing should he, as would be only natural, mistake it for a graceful token of absentee hospitality—and of myself arraigned for manslaughter.

"For God's sake, don't drink anything out of any kind of bottle in that flat," I wrote him immediately. "It might kill you."

"Dear Mrs. Jones: However do you think I am comporting myself in your home," Insel answered. "Were there thirty bottles of the finest schnapps I should not touch them. Rest assured you will find your apartment *exactly* as you left it."

He sounded quite comfortably settled. I had also written him to get my charwoman to clean his suit with odorless gasoline at my expense, and inquired how much money he had left.

"Your suggestion for my suit is most kind—

however, I am convinced that it is only on account of the dirt in it that it still holds together."

He had, he said, enough money to last him for a "little" week.

We had agreed that I should come every few days for a dressmaker's fitting at the further end of the flat where it would not disturb him. When I did go, a bewildered concierge informed me, "Madame, the artist who was to live in your apartment never came."

"That only means he has not yet been 'turned out,' " I explained to her, while to myself I reflected, "You will find your apartment exactly . . . the monkey!"

I felt that the end of his little week was no longer my concern, and I forgot all about him.

I would run into Paris for the dressmaker, a tea, a dinner and back to my little hotel in St. Cloud again, until at last the time drew near for exporting pictures—among them were to be included some of Insel's.

"Pictures, drawings, three o'clock," I wired him. At a quarter past, he had not arrived and I went to tea with a friend who hailed me from the courtyard, leaving a note on the door, "Will be back shortly."

When I returned the place was different—in the smoothed out air there was a suspicion of a collapse in time. As if by a magnet, I was drawn into the studio and up to the dark oak table. Upon it lay a flat packet. I could have sworn it emitted a faint phosphorescence that advanced from all the rest of the room. The wrapping paper was so strikingly creaseless it looked unusual. It had in some inexplicable manner become precious as ivory; its squareness was instinctively exact as the hexagons of wasps.

"He has left the drawings," I supposed, almost reluctantly undoing this magnetic focus of an uncanny precision. But once unfolded, I found it contained only a shabby block of writing paper that had been left lying there and from which I had torn the note I left for him.

"Did you find anything?" he asked when, later having resuscitated from the moribund state in which he preferred to arrive, he was able to articulate.

"Yes. What on earth—?"

"I wrapped it up," said Insel—an enormous intention fixed in his eyes.

It was at this moment that, for me, Insel, from a seedy man, dissolved into a strange mirage, the only thing in the world at that time to stir my curiosity.

On his arrival with the pictures he had appeared the phantom of himself as I had seen him last. He had so weakened, become so transparent.

Deeply bowed, he clutched his feeble fist in the emptiness where his stomach should have been. From this profound concavity arose a dying whimper of, "Water—*aspirine*," as out of the abdominal void rode the unclenching fist—his tremulous fingers, hovering over the bureau, grasped a cigarette.

"Well, you're in a nice state," I taunted him to cover my alarmed compassion. "Why didn't you write?"

He gulped his *aspirine* as if to alleviate a death rattle. "I did write."

"Yes, a comic strip. I found my flat *exactly* as I left it."

"I know," said Insel, gently abashed. "I ought to have told you 'I am not here.' "

"Even the least of philanthropists," I laughed, "has sensibilities—I thought I had been intrusive. You see, Insel, any possible gesture in the face of poverty must inevitably be insolent, its very necessity—in not being outs—makes poverty so aloof."

"And I thought you were *angry* because I mentioned money."

"I had *told* you to mention money. But all my sympathy for you was buried under that bunch of cheap flowers I put here to welcome the lonely *clochard*."

"But, after all, I have been here nearly every day," he almost sobbed, "to look for you. I could never find you. I knew when you had been here for where you trod there lay little fragments of stuff. I could trace your movements by the pins you shed on the floor. Think what it was like—to seek after a woman, a vanishing woman, and in her stead, to find nothing but pins," he implored. Then brightening, "I picked them all up. Look," said Insel, hurriedly reversing the lapel of his jacket. On the underside stuck in rows as precise as in packages from the factory, were my dressmaker's fallen pins. He dropped the lapel into place again as if too long he had bared this precious hoard of his compelling exactitude.

With an interminable cautiousness Insel had revived. "*Ich bin nicht fromm—*I am not pious," he mused, deeply introspective. "And yet how I have prayed, I prayed," he burst out, a blind agony falling upon his eyes, "I prayed that you would come back!"

"You seem to have been thinking about me a good deal—hadn't you any steak?"

"I never *cease* thinking of you," he muttered, as if fearful I should overhear—and aloud, "None," he answered flatly yet without reproach.

As mediums on becoming professional, obliged to continuate an intermittent condition, lapse to the most lamentable dupery, Insel would actually plagiarize his innate mediumistic quality of which he appeared to be but partially conscious.

It would seem unnecessary after the intrinsic wizardry of his simple packet to resort to the untenable mystery of a lie. Yet he did.

Awestricken, solemn, he recounted to me that while I had, as it were, struck myself off his menu, Mlle Alpha had sent him a card to know how he was getting on.

"The world is populated with people anxious to know how I am getting on. But when I tell them— the world immediately depopulates! I wrote her in answer, 'Am starving to death except for a miracle

—three o'clock Tuesday afternoon will be the end.'
—And then your telegram! for three o'clock. Today is Tuesday.

"Of course she did not answer," he commented, "I had rather thought she might be good for fifty francs. Nobody ever sends one fifty francs," he ended despondently.

"Oh, *what's* the matter with you, Insel? That girl has more sex appeal than almost anyone in Paris. And all your reaction is that she might be good for fifty francs. I never could interpret, until I saw her, the French, *Elle n'a pas froid aux yeux*—the Alpha's eyes are volcanic. All the men are in love with her."

"Not I," he boasted.

"No-o? I should say that clochards were hardly in her line."

"Grade—exactly," Insel concurred as if relieved of a responsibility.

Characteristically, after swearing he would ask her for his card as proof of a miraculous coincidence with his usual unconcern in breaking up his plots it was Insel who insisted on my meeting Mlle Alpha whom I knew only slightly.

5

FLEISCH ohne Knochen," Insel especially hollow-voiced begged me when I took him to dine. This insistence on boneless pieces of meat was habitual with him.

"Do I look any fatter?" he inquired after he had eaten, as if consulting his doctor.

I thought it best to reply in the affirmative. As a matter of fact the disquieting thing about Insel was that however much food you sunk in him it no more seemed to amalgamate with him than would a concrete mass with a gaseous compound.

From now on Insel turned up regularly as soon as my fitting by the dressmaker was over.

Whenever I let him in he would halt on the threshold drawing the whole of his luminous life up into his smile. It radiated round his face and formed a halo hovering above the rod of his rigid body. He looked like a lamppost alight. Perhaps in that moment before the door opened he recreated himself out of a nothingness into which he must relapse when being alone his magnetism had no one to contact.

"I've brought 'it,' " his illusive grin seemed to

be announcing, as if his visible person were a mannequin he operated on occasion. "Make what you can of it—you may wonder if I am sure of its nature myself—let us not be too precise as to what I am."

I led him down the corridor, feeling that he, so recently non-existent, was all-surprised at finding himself to be anything at all.

He shut the door, an act I have heard an authoress describe as so banal it is unfit for publication. But shutting the door, like all automatism we take for granted, is stupendous in its implications.

As the ancients built temples as isolators for the power of the Almighty, which their ritual focused on the altar, a force so dynamic that officiating priests, having evoked it, were constrained to descend the altar steps backwards without ceasing to face it; for the limitless capacity of the eyes could absorb such power, whereas if the blind back were turned upon it they would receive a shock that flung them to the ground.

So the shutting of doors is a concentration of our radiations in rectangular containers, to economize the essences of our being we dispense to those with whom we communicate.

Thus, when Insel shut the door infinitesimal currents ran out of him into the atmosphere as if he were growing a soft invisible fur that, when reciprocal conditions were sufficiently suave, grew longer and longer as the hair of the dead, it is maintained, will leisurely fill a coffin until it seemed with its measured infiltration even to interfere with Time. The mesmeric rhythm of a film slowed down conducted the tempo of thought and sentience in response to his half-petrified tepidity, for he moved within an outer circle of partial decease—a ring of death surrounding him—that reminded one of those magically animated corpses described by William Seabrook. Even before he came into one's presence, one received a draughty intimation of his frosty approach. He chilled the air, flattened the hour, faded color.

But if one could crash through this necrophilous aura, its consistency dissolved, one came to an inner circle where serial things floated in a semi-existent aquarium. Or, at times he, himself, would overflood it, as now when his coming close to me affected acclimatization, turning an irreal ice into a tenuous warmth.

"I was so terribly afraid I should miss you. I got to bed at seven this morning—(quite exceptional," he added hurriedly as if wishing to efface a bad impression, "I shall not do it again), and when I woke up my watch said twenty past six. I was convinced you would be gone, but—is it not astounding—a moment later it said half past four."

To these teeny nothings that marked out his life (as momentous events are the milestones of others) he imparted an interest peculiarly visual. You saw the watch in hallucinatory transformation, its dial advancing the gray diamonds of his eyes out of a murk more mysterious than darkness instead of correcting the eyes' mistake. He possessed some mental conjury enabling him to infuse an actual detail with the magical contrariness surrealism merely portrays. Perhaps it was the operation of this weird power that necessitated his speaking with such drilling intensity.

He had brought me a present— As he bowed his head over what he held in his hands, all the sweet-stuffs of the earth exuded from his nerves, in an exquisite music of a silence that is alive. He seemed to be sodden with some ineffable satisfaction, as if emerged drenched from some luxuriance requiring little tangible for its consummation. I had to hold myself in check. My charmed curiosity wanted to cry, "From what enchanted bed of love have you so lately arisen? What astral Venus has just receded from your embrace?"

It was a queer impulse, the idea of making such delicious inquiry of this bald and toothless man whose clothes were stiff with years of wear, yet deodorized by continuous exposure to the all-night air.

His voice, gone dim with a crushed emotion as he held out to me a black passe-partout, was saying, "I want to give you my own drawing; the only one I refuse to sell." The drawing in the passe-partout, like his atmosphere that clung to him as ours clings to the earth, seemed almost astir with that somnolent arrested motion revealing his nature.

It was so white, the flocking skies of a strangely disturbing purity drifted above vortices of snow-like mist in travail of taking shape, coiling the mind into following the spiral, eventual materialization of blindly virginal elementals.

"This," he continued, "is the first drawing of a new series—all my future work will be based on it. I intend my technique to become more and more minute, until, the grain becoming entirely invisible, it will look like a photograph. Then, when my monsters do evolve, they will create the illusion that they really exist; that they *have* been photographed."

The while the drift of his words swept me together with the frozen drawing along a current of quiet reverence, expressing gratitude. As under his conjurative power of projecting images, I felt myself grow to the ruby proportions of a colossal beef steak.

I argued for some time over the idiocy of presents in the very jaws of economic death; proposed sending it to New York to be sold for him; but at length when he inquired sadly, "It doesn't please you? I will give you another," I promised to keep it.

6

I'M SO UGLY NAKED," he told me most unexpectedly, in a tone of intense and anxious confidence. "I can't go to the public baths because I daren't walk down to the water."

"Your face is naked and you walk about with it."

"Yes," he assented miserably, "and it frightens the women. I used to be so beautiful. Is it imaginable?" he asked, peering expectantly into my face.

"I'm tired of your tirade as to how hideous you are."

"All women are terrified of me," he continued automatically.

"I said tired—not terrified, and I'll tell you why. I've never really seen you. You always give me the impression that you are *not there*. Sometimes you have no inside; sometimes no outside, and never enough of anything to entirely materialize. Like a quicksand, when one looks at you whatever one gets a glimpse of you immediately rush up from your own depths to snatch. *Your* way of being alive is a sequence of disappearances. You're so afraid of actuality."

"I can materialize for *you*," he said raptly, "*forever*—on the corner of this street."

Somehow we were sitting on the Terrasse of the Hotel Lutetia. It stood behind us dressed in its name of a pagan Paris. It might very well be actually surviving for our blind backs which, taking no part in the present, are carried around with us as if concrete in the past.

Darting about amazingly in the autumn vapor innumerable metal beetles of various species with which modern man, still unable to create soft-machines and so limited to the construction of heavy plagiarisms that sometimes crush him, had sprinkled the *carrefour* facing us, where gasoline impregnating the dust had begotten a vitiated yet exhilarating up-to-date breath of life.

A distant gnat of a thousand horsepower hummed in the heavens.

"If only we could sit here eternally it would be *wunderbar*—it's just like sitting in the kitchen."

"The kitchen?" I exclaimed.

"Ah, yes," he sighed. "All my youth I ate in the kitchen together with my *Vater und Mutter* and the other five children." Then, inhaling the effluvia of the streets, "There was lots of steam," he said invigorated. "All the washing hung up to dry, the muddy boots stood in a row, and on the good hot stove—"

"*Die Suppe*," I joined in, entranced.

"*Ja, die Suppe*," he confirmed ecstatically. "You see, it is not so much a matter of materializing but of being able to speak. Before I found you I had never anyone I could speak to. I should never have been able to tell about all this—"

"All the boots?" I interrupted.

"—to anyone else," he concluded, his voice trailing off as if calling to me from another world.

"*Allein—allein*," he chanted forsakenly. Something was happening to this man's voice, the most musical modulations were stealing into it. "Always alone—alone in Berlin—alone in Paris—" The words floated out of him like wisps of a dream, "more than alone in prison."

"In prison," I responded, "where there is no one,

no one you can convince of your not being there. You might try it on the warden, but the moment he began to suspect would be the very moment he assured himself of your presence—I mean—let's leave that and have something more to eat!"

In sitting so close to Insel at the small terrace table all the filaments of what has been called the astral body, that network of vibrational force, were being drawn out of me towards a terrific magnet, while I sat unmoved beside the half-rotten looking man of flesh. My astral inclination, withheld by a counteractive physical repulsion, could not gain its presumable end of flying onto that magnet— It was as though he had achieved an impossible confusion of his positive and negative polarity— Out of a dim past echoed the din of a music hall refrain I had heard in Berlin: "*Du musst herüber—*You must come over."

7

THE LESS HE SEEMED TO BE "there," the more he spilled into the unknown, the more clearly I apprehended him, whereas Insel himself seemed ever to be seeking a reduction of focus through which to penetrate into the real world.

Suddenly he bowed his head over me in a wracking attentiveness. He had found such a focus. Darting, his constricted fingers cleaved to a white hair of my head which had fallen on my coat, he made a ritual of offering it to my eyes.

"*Je suis la ruine féerique,*" I trilled in vanity.

"Ah, yes," sighed Insel, as I translated, churning me with his eyes into the colorless vapors of his creation.

The cloth of my coat, a *fantaisie*, was sewn with lacquered red setae—wisps, scarcely attached, which caught the light, and all through the evening unusual manifestations of consciousness occurring outside the Lutetia were punctuated by Insel's staccato spoliation of that hairy cloth. He could not desist. Like an adult elf insanely delousing a mortal, whenever I laughingly reprimanded him for ruining my coat, with an acrid cluck of refutation he would show me what he had instantly plucked from the cloth—it was always a *white* hair— He did not trouble to contradict me—the evidence was clinching— But in the end the side of my coat sitting next to him was bare of all its fancy setae.

In accordance with the rules of sympathetic magic, so long concealing my one fallen hair in his palm augmented Insel's influence over me. An influence which, rather than having submitted to it, I purposely invaded, so urgent was my premonition of some treasure he contained. His voice now setting in a glowing duskiness haunted me with wonder as to where I had heard it before—

"Black as was the stain on my name—," I listened to Insel intoning as if he were celebrating mass, "even so white would I wash it in glory—."

Rising for a moment from the fantastic shallows of his cerebral proximity to my normal level, "This man is *fearfully* banal," I said to myself, discerning in his confidences the prim hypocrisy of a wastrel bamboozling the patroness of some charitable institution. Any such patroness would have cried for help should she receive him as he was at present plunged in the depths of a subverted exaltation, so awesomely he stressed his lonely agony, his long starvation, the incidentless introspection of that enjailed jewel, his artist spirit. As for me, the fundamental lacuna in my experience was being "stopped up" with his moral man. The pattern held out to my early ethical life. The man who stones. He who unsuspectingly lingers in the world subconscious.

I did not care whom he bamboozled. Slipping back into his sensitized zone, I swallowed his platitudes gratefully. So seldom had I come across *anything* sufficiently *condensed* to satisfy my craving for "potted absolute." This man sufficed me as representing all the hungry errantry of the human race.

"What are you trying to be anyhow?" I asked bemused. "*La faim qui rode autour des palaces?*"

A sound of anguish was hovering above us but I scarcely registered it listening to his quiet soliloquy in reverence for the buried aspiration whence sprung the weedy heroism of his pretence.

"Dolefully trite in his insincerity," my common sense intervened.

"Inflexible is his moral will," countered the underside of my mentality which drawing comparisons to sociologists' deceptions in criminal reform preferred to remain impressed.

"*Der edler Mensch,*" it breathed devoutly, "The noble creature."

Still looking so extraordinarily distinguished, Insel was illustrating a society by means of an empty plate, a diaphragm reducing the world to a white spot.

"There are *you*—" pointing the tip of his nose toward the center—a comical almost four-cornered tip of a nose with the sudden sharpness of a (square tool, the name of which I have forgotten), "and here am I—on the outside—peeping over the edge at you," he said as he crept his fingers in their incipient movement up from under the rim.

I was disappointed. One thing about Insel that had struck me was this sporadic distinction I had often been "accused" of which I had always been eager to discover in anyone else who, like myself, had "popped up" from nowhere at all—as if all my life I had lacked a crony of my "own class."

I could not point this out. It would upset Insel's self-abasement which gave him some mysterious satisfaction—as of an Olympian in masquerade—

That sound above, once it hooked up with perception, became a squirling wail—soaring over the driving racket of the street corner.

"Do you hear?" asked Insel, "it's been going on for quite a while—in an aerial invasion people would sit on at their cafe tables just as we have done. Air raids," he shuddered, shrinking into himself, "and the French so proud of their Maginot Line. They have forgotten *their* Stavisky was mixed up with it— Sugar," beamed Insel, a gentle delirium stealing into his eyes, "tons and tons of sugar poured into the foundations of the Maginot Line."

"Sugar's rather expensive," I ventured.

"Nevertheless," averred Insel, and I felt it might be perilous to contradict him.

His chuckle petered out as the siren insinuating to his brain the menace of a war which would cut off any chuckling, transformed it to a shudder.

Insel trembled with the cowardice of those whose instinct being to create even an iota, appear to slink into a corner before the heroic of destructive intent. This man, who, when he turned his face full on you, looked into your eyes with the great intensity of the hypnotist but with a force of concentration reaching inward and outward as if he must first subject himself to his own mysterious influence, this man in his terror had dropped from his own magnetic "line" soft as a larva. He cowered against the air. Inasmuch as it concerned him, war was not only imminent—he was already ripped open by its plough of anguish. Actually, he was in a fix—for, in the "event" being a German, here he was an enemy, whereas if he could return to Germany, there he was *Kultur Bolshewik.*

Man Ray came up and sat with us and went away. Tables filled and emptied. The dust grew denser and then lay down before the oncoming night.

I once heard somebody express surprise that instead of following it onward one should not take a cut across Time to secure a moment which, stretching out in line with oneself, would last indefinitely.

Time that evening lightly came to rest—an unburdened nomad let its three faces linger; the future and the past were with me at present: the whole of time—there was no more pursuing it, losing it, regretting it—while I sat almost shoulder to shoulder with this virtual stranger living the longest period of my life.

It is almost impossible to recover the sequence or the veritable simultaneity of the states of consciousness one experienced in the company of this uncommon derelict. It was so very much as if consciousness was performing stunts. Always in his vicinity one had the impression of living in or rather of being surrounded by an arid aquarium—filled with, not water, but a dim transparency: the pro-creational chaotic vapor in which all things may begin to grow.

Either he had a peculiar power of projecting his visualizations or some leak in his psyche enabled you to tap the half formulated concepts that drifted through his mind: glaucous shades dissolved and deepened into the unreal tides of an ocean without waves. Where in the bottom of slumber an immobile oncome of elementals formed of a submarine snow, and some aflicker, like drowned diamonds blew out their rudimentary bellies—almost protruded foetal arms over all an aimless baton of inaudible orchestra—a colorless water-plant growing the stumpy battlements of a castle in a game of chess waved in and out of perceptibility its vaguely phallic reminder—.

Projected effigies of Insel and myself insorcellated flotsam—never having left any land—never to arrive at any shore—static in an unsuspected magnitude of being alive in the "light of the eye" dilated to an all enclosing halo of unanalyzable insight, where wonder is its own revelation.

Even in the world of reality Insel's ideation was an introvert exploration of a brilliancy beneath his skull, an ever-crescent clarity which in the form of inspiration ripens creative fruit. But in him by reason of some interference I could not define, aborted as the introduction to an idea.

"I can see right into these people," he asserted, indicating the crowd gathered around the Hotel. "I know exactly what they are; I know what they do."

And that was all.

As if satisfied by his sense of insight, he needed not to perceive anything specifically, his mind exposed these people as brightly illuminated "whats." A reaction he accepted for entire comprehension.

His conceptions were like seeds fallen upon an iron girder. I noticed that I received them very much in the guise of photographic negatives so hollow and dusky they became in transmission, vaguely accentuated with inverted light—.

Thus, as he unfolded his ardent yearning to flee to New York from a threatening war, the transparencies his presence superposed on the living scene became crowded with flimsy skyscrapers. Up from among their floating foundations swam misty negresses, their limbs spread out at inviting angles, like starfish through the mirage of windows plunging in fathomless pools their reflections.

But this is not all that happened with him. The visions emitted by the organism of this truly congenital surrealist were only a wasted pollen drifting off from the nuclear flower of his identity. For my first unaccountable conclusion that he was "the most delicate—soul," my fascinated impression of his emergence from a goddess' embrace, the dove that, when he had been still for a while would seem to take his place, were conceptions fully justified by the lovely equilibrium his companionship conveyed to me. It was as if for an exceeding moment I could, rising above the distortion of life, hold inexpressible communion with Insel, where his spirit had no flaw.

Within range of the crystalline of his eyes become so brightly brittle, again I experienced the profound relief of the acute celerity rhythm that perpetually disintegrated me as I got out of watching a film in slow motion.

Imagining aloud the explorative kick of roaming the mountainous blocks of Manhattan "forever in New York—," Insel chanted, "we could have such a wonderful time together." He was not speaking. He was praying.

Idly I wondered with what he was communicating, when suddenly I felt myself sag; become so spineless, so raw—. I, a red island with its shores of suet, the most dependable substance in an aquarium-America not so very much dimmer than the Paris cars threading through it in the Rue de Sèvres.

I did not find it extraordinary that my condition as an undiminishable steak should make me feel almost sublime, or that the man intensely leaning towards me should pray to it.

There was another element in his unbelievable magnetism of recoil. His air of friability warning off contact lest he crumble. Not only was he preposterously emaciated, but even as his gravity seemed lightened, his body—what was left of it—seemed less ponderable than it should have been. Insel was made of extremely diaphanous stuff. Between the shrunken contour of his present volume his original "serial mold" was filled in with some intangible aural matter remaining in place despite his anatomical shrinkage. An aura that enveloped him with an extra external sensibility.

To investigate, I tapped him lightly on the arm in drawing his attention—and actually in a tenuous way I did feel my hand pass through "something." The surface of his cloth sleeve, like a stiff sieve, was letting that something through. The effect on Insel was unforeseeable—jerking his face over his shoulder, he twitched away from my fingers with the acid sneer of a wounded feline. This might be merely a reflex of physical repulsion to myself, so later I repeated the gesture, but as if my hand in its first contact had got coated with the psychic exudence it would seem there was no longer any hurt in it. He was calm under my touch.

8

THE REVERSE OF HIS ALOOFNESS was a hollow invitation to my intrusion. Urged to cross the frontier of his individuality, I got in the way of that faintly electric current he emitted. His magnetic pull steadily on the increase, the repulsion proportionately defined, threw me into a vibrational quandary, until as if it were imperative for me to make a connection with the emissive agency of my accidental clairvoyance, with a supernormal acumen he inspired, I located the one point of contact: the temple. Straightway I found myself possessed of an ability to form a "mental double" (for no portion of my palpable substantiality was in any way involved), a mental double of my own temple.

This was one manifestation of how in Insel's

vicinity pieces of bodies would seem to break off as astral fractions and on occasion hang, visually suspended in the air. Quite apparently to my subconscious the bit of my skull encaving the fragile area flew off me, crashed onto his and stuck there.

On the spur of this subvoluntary cohesion to the telepathic center—I definitely penetrated (into) his mediumistic world where illusory experience which had so far escaped as scarcely whispered pictures took on a fair degree of resemblance to three-dimensional concretion: the sculpture of hallucination succeeding to the visionary film.

Insel straightened as a water level, his petrified eyes drilling the image of his coma into the ultimate ceiling, broke into a right angle of prostration and ascension.

Out of a torso of white ash arose iron rags as puffs of curling smoke, blocks of shadow crushed together in the outline of a giant. Dense as the dark, high as a tower, the almost imperceptible radiance of a will-o'-the-wisp shining from it—I crouched alongside encumbered with an enormous shell white as plaster which, having but partly taken shape, trailed to an end in a sail of mist.

And all the while Insel kept up his mixture of *Beggar's Opera* and oratorio, showing a tragi-comic duality in his confidences. A coxcomb in purgatory, he enlivened a suppliant self-abasement with pranks he was proud to have played on a short-sighted mistress. Vast tracks of his barren universe were fixed in her monocle.

Our discussions of his tribulations had the light hilarity of conversation between clowns. Our shoulders almost touching, we seemed to have come within risible distance of each other. As if our imbecilic mirth were due to an assurance that suffering loses weight when tossed to and fro.

Intermittently his intriguing anxieties ceased to be actual. In his cerebral commotion, Trouble, attaining an inflation at which it burst, had no further existence except in the fragments constituting his exhortations for help which, at that, were his means of entertaining one.

Albert Londres tells of a lunatic who periodically would drop whatever he was doing to go up to the wall and say peculiar prayers to it. So Insel had two or three intimate anecdotes he had to "get off." He told them whenever I met him with an earnestness that, like a gentle gimlet, bored into my mind. The culminative point of his corporeal life had been his threat to shoot a girl who left him for a lesbian, and of his psychic life, his magnetic rays drawing some other girl out of bed on to her balcony whenever he passed below at night.

As a prayer, repeated over and over, becoming autohypnotic, attains to faith in each retelling, these stories grew vaster, lasted longer, reached farther into a kind of absolute of confidence. As if with incantations he must summon up his past because some unimaginable impediment withheld the present and the future from him. His mind besieged the barred outlet of today-into-tomorrow in an effort to break it down and gather fresh material, but on finding itself impotent revoked to memory, dilating his souvenirs until for him the story of the universe was blotted out by the gigantism of his meager individual experience.

Externally his aspect was vague as, internally, the rudimentary ideas stored in his cerebral cells. His person withdrawing in approaching, his eyes appeared to start their staring in advance of the brows that encaved them. Between his "expression" preceding his face and his speech which so often sounded as if issuing from a distance behind him, his person melted from view. In him everything seemed inverted. His voice in its drilling intensity getting softer, louder, would go up higher, lower.

My casual ability to partake of his moods evoked my own anxiety of the past which joining in his terror of the aerial omen made it doubly real. The nomistic warning which recurred to my mind, "He who looks back returns to the maze," I disobeyed; so intense was my intuitional curiosity as to the leak in Insel's magnetic coherence. I felt that giving in to a dislocation of my identity, which is usually perilous or demoralizing, must in this exceptional case, be finally vindicated by a revelation of what supremely lovely essence was being conveyed to me by this human wreck. In the light of this my certitude his corporeal mendicancy appeared fictitious. So surely it was an exquisite nucleus that in his somewhat comatose exaltation he struggled to save. On the instant I accepted this

salvation as equally my affair. Memory in euthan-
asia will come to life when fed on the same sort of
stuff as that which formed it—.

Insel, the animate cadaver, stretched with the
pliancy of decay from the last war into the next—
while walls of solid murder with soldiers for bricks
came marching in on a living aspiration—to enclose
it—waste it—it must not happen again.

"*Vielleicht verkaufen,*" I could hear Insel mut-
tering as I made this decision, obsessed by an impersonal responsibility. He was toting up imaginary
accounts in payment of his passage to America.

"Promise to be my guide and companion?" he
implored earnestly while staring straight before him
as if it did not matter where I was.

"How tedious," my everyday self recoiled, the
lovely essence evaporating, for whenever Insel
turned his profile he sort of extinguished. It was only when both his eyes were fixed upon me I entered
his Edenic region of unreasoning bliss to sway
among immaterial algae.

In profile, as if he cut himself in half and in halv-
ing should leave himself evil, he became so alien,
so very elfin, he induced aversion. The notch at the
spring of the nose was further back than the drop
of the upper lip. These angles of his pasty face were
over-acute and out of plumb. A kink near the ear
suggested the wire-hung jaw of a ventriloquist's
dummy. In profile, this nitwit infused with the secret
ghost, seemed to have been carved for a joke out
of moldy wood.

"*Immer—immer spazieren*—eternally taking a walk," he insisted, once more aware of my presence; his voice dwindled to a pathos so unearthly it could only converse with the unconscious. His eyes, for dusk had fallen, were phosphorescent as approaching fireflies.

As Insel consecrated our spontaneous comradeship with his tom-tom reiterations of how he delighted to talk to me, and I, nonplussed, would hazily inquire, "What about?" I kept on naming him to myself.

"*Die nackte Seele,*" and again, "*Die nackte Seele.*"

It seemed quite fortuitous that sitting beside him I should feel I was up against "the naked soul." Practically anything might substitute in my consciousness for a man, who, however long I looked at him I could never entirely "put together."

We had been sitting outside the Lutetia for six hours.

"Now," laughed Insel, "Man Ray should pass again."

"To conclude, we have no use for time."

"That is not what I mean—"

"You mean that eternity spins round and round?"

We arose. But our legs become paralyzed from sitting so long on the hard little chairs, we barely saved ourselves from toppling over and staggered across the pavement. Suddenly the Metro opened at my feet. In the midst of a sentence I dropped from sight as if impelled to conform with Insel's concepts by flickering out. One seldom took leave of him; (walking along with him one would unexpectedly drift sideways into a cab) as Insel, in an electric sputter, softly mumbled "*schade.*"

So now I descended the stairway—Insel leaned over it in his disgraceful grace, "When shall I see you again?" he implored, clutching his concave breast. An awesome lunar reflection lit up his face from within.

9

ON ONE OF MY VISITS to town Insel did not turn up, but when I left home to dine with friends I met him drifting round the corner with the wild concern of having too lately thrown off an unguessable inertia.

He greeted me with the relief of an object which, having fallen apart, should chance upon its other half again. His discomforting friable surface had slightly embodied; he even—I felt, but was not sure—took my arm: a brittle elbowing into the prelude of some *danse macabre.*

With a kind of epileptic cajolery he beseeched me to break my appointment. Finding this ghostly courtesy agreeable as any other, I decided to give him half an hour. I would drive to my friends instead of walking. So down we sat to suffuse another stray cafe with the ineffable haze of his contagion.

Insel, leaning back against his chair in a tall recline of felicity, groped in his pocket and took out something I could not see for he held it like a conjuror. Signing for me to hold out my hand he placed his over it as a cupola showering so discreet a sensitiveness my hand responded as a plot of invisible grasses grazed by an imperceptible breath.

"The girl," he whispered, and the grasses parted under a couple of atomies cupped in my palm; Insel and his girl embracing—or were they Adam and Eve? "The girl gave me this," he said, puckering his face in helpless incomprehension. "And it won't go."

I looked at what he had dropped in my hand—a sordid silver watch on a worn leather strap.

"Will you take it to be mended?" he wooed me. "You can speak French."

As soon as I was seated beside him I had reached the extremity of optimism. The landscape of a spattered hoarding across the street was too lovely to look at. I had to lower my eyelids. Insel already had lowered his on a face falling lower and lower into the excavation of his breast.

He started up, elated to impart what he had found there. Evidently a death warrant.

"I am to die," he rejoiced. "And will you weep one little tear for me?" he asked flirtatiously.

"Yum, yum," I jibed, intent on the beauty of the silver rivers he had loosened in the veins of the ugly marble table top. "Does ums want to be pitied?—you've struck a hunk of granite."

"You *won't* weep?" he implored from a gust of sad laughter.

"Not a drop."

Insel tried again. "*Sterben,*" he sighed in the voice of a weary archangel, an incommemorable voice burying the endlessness of death in two syllables. I was disturbed—if he should peter out on that annihilating refrain I would never know what was so weirdly, so wonderfully the matter with this exquisite scarecrow.

"Insel," I shook him gently, "you're much more likely to make people weep by remaining alive."

But Insel, passionately in love with Death, raved in a soft, a sublime sibilance, "*Sterben—man muss—man—mu—uss.*" This fair decease in which he infinitely delighted, vaster and more dimly distant than the lesser deaths of his usual aberrations, sailed with Insel on its wings to heights of a stratospheric purity.

At once the hoarding became abominable, the marble of the table the color of nausea, the whole of the world depressing, and Insel, a dilapidated suicide, hung aloft from a terrifyingly rusty nail together with all his unpainted pictures—. This was a recollection of the somber ambition which stirred him whensoever he became aware of his real life. It looked pretty bad—real life—so carelessly repaired by hand—that obscene, that relentless hoarding. Insel, his eyes closed upon it, induced by Death the absolute decoy, examined an integral vision lining the degeneracy of his brain.

His dirge still hummed on the air—.

Life without world, how starkly lovely, stripped of despair. The soul, inhabiting the body of an ethic, ascended to the sapphire in the attic. Here was no need for salvage. If he preferred to attain perfection, I would let Insel loose to die as he pleased. But my unconscious, with an inkling of what perfection was like after sharing to some degree in his increate Eden, squirmed with envy.

If Insel committed suicide—I could share in that, too. My envy at once supplanted by a flowering peace—filling with fragrance—space. Through a break in the cool white blot of its branches—I perceived the cafe clock. On that uncompromising dial all things converged to normal. I was a tout for a friend's art gallery, feeding a cagey genius in the hope of production. Insel's melodious ravings, an irritating whine— It was ten to eight.

Nevertheless, as Insel was going to *sterben*—the word now sounded flatly banal—I promised to meet him at the Dôme after the cinema. "Take this," I said. "Be sure you eat a wholesome meal," with my usual mental ejection of the obvious man, to whom I was definitely averse.

This unreasonable nonchalant faith in Insel's alter ego was about to be greatly rewarded. After my amusing dinner and a good film which, when we came out, proved to have lasted much longer than usual, on our return in my friends' car the lightning hand of pain unexpectedly grabbed my internal organs and, twisting them in a grim convulsion, wrung out of them as from a dishrag a deathly inner perspiration—as if one were about to retch a nothingness poisoned with anguish. I was in for it, this being the preliminary to invasion by the tenacious rodent which would not cease from me for days.

It was one o'clock and Insel might have waited since half past eleven. He had. When my friends in some concern dropped me at the Dôme I could see him sitting outside.

Insel seemed unconscious of having waited for me for an hour and a half. After all it was ridiculous stopping to apologize to one who lived in that other time and space. My reflection immediately complicated, "When was he here? When was he there? Was he in a wavering way existing in both dimensions at once?" The distant aristo went about his simple social life with sufficient consecutiveness, save for long delays excused with mysterious illness and misplaced sleep, he visited anyone who would have him on the right day.

During my absence he had changed.

I had never seen him like this before—human—actually gay! As I tried to explain why I must go home, Insel, in laughing over something he wanted to tell me, laid a fluttering hand on my shoulder—the torture of my body ceased.

It was not only an interruption of pain. I was regalvanized. Straightening from top to toe, I inhaled a limpid air—the neon tubes caressed my eyes.

I looked at Insel amazed. In what unheard of parasitism had I drawn this vitality out of a creature half-disintegrated?

Evidently he was in good form. The sparks he seemed to emit in turn gave off smaller ones; an added superficial illumination induced by a few drinks, having much the same effect as the perspective confusion of traffic lights among electric signs.

Out of all this an intimate twinkle approached me. "Promise to sit here with me till seven o'clock tomorrow evening," Insel entreated.

"Naturally," I acquiesced.

There is no field of fantasy so rich as the financial promoting of failures. Weaving in and out of our conversation was a shuttle of money-making devices for Insel's relief, the most practical being to star him in a horror film. It is a poor horror which has to grime its face—the only face on the films that has true horror in it is Jouvet's—and that only an inkling—and so discreet.

Insel said he had been offered such a role. But again he had not been able, or wishful, to pursue anything that carried him into the future—a future that ebbed from him as from others the past. He would look forward with one eagerly—always at a certain point he reverted—turned his blind back on the forward direction—.

He said, "I have worn myself out tramping the city on fruitless quests—to show my good will."

Now I had found another profession for him— magnetic healer. Suddenly I foresaw the fear my physician would inspire nullifying his therapeutic value, and I did not suggest it to Insel.

In his unusual liveliness, words, like roomy cupboards, dipped into the reservoir of excited honey and flapping their open doors spilled it all over the place as they passed.

"*Unglaublich,*" said Insel. "With you alone am I able to express myself. You tell me exactly what I am thinking. No one else has understood what we understand.

"You have such marvelous ideas—"

"But Insel," I protested conscientiously, "I have touched on my ideas so lightly— If I knew your language well enough to convey the subtlest shades of meaning—."

We decided to get a first-class dictionary. Henceforth *nothing* was to be lost!

Summing it up, this unspecific converse whose savor lay in its impress of endlessness has left me an ineradicable visual definition of Insel with his whittled exterior jerking in tics of joy a pate too loosely attached and almost worn down to the skull—and myself expansive in some secondary glow from that icy conflagration strewing gray ashes over his face as it burnt itself out. Always at an instinctive interval of shoulder from shoulder, as two aloft on the same telegraph wire exchange a titter of godforsaken sparrows.

As night drew out—it got draftier and draftier— we removed, as if receding into a lair, from the terrace to further and further inside the cafe, from the open to the enclosed—each time ordering a new *consommation* from a different waiter—till we reached an inaereate core of the establishment. Here we inexplicably came upon that friend whose hypothetic non-existence insured Insel's vaunted isolation. One after another the same Germanic wag would shuffle up to our table, each time wearing a different face.

One—projected that declamatory arm which in a certain condition present at the time falls with a forgetful plop before completing an indication. "Who is Insel," it challenged, "to monopolize this perfectly fascinating woman?"

Another—equally appreciative until he discovered the hair in the shadow of my hat to be undeniably white—apologized with a shudder, "I won't say it doesn't look all right on you—but I can't bear the sight. It reminds me that *I* am old." He looked less old than Insel— He was one of the many unfortunates who have had nothing to "give off" but the bubbles of adolescence, whereas Insel's rattling pelvis was trotting the leather seat in the sitting leaps of an exuberant child.

"They are so surprised," he chortled repeatedly. "They are accustomed to seeing me *all alone*—."

I ordered supper—got cigarettes at the counter and dumped them on our table on my way downstairs to buy some rouge (probably on a cue my subconscious had taken from my critic). When I returned it looked as if the empty space in our quiet corner had come alive, the leather padding had broken out in a parasitic formation, a double starfish whose radial extremities projected and retracted rapidly at dynamic angles.

It was Insel all cluttered up with his "private life." Draped with the bodies of two negresses, spiked with their limbs. They seemed, out of ambush, to have fallen upon him from over the back of the high seat. The waiter had laid a startling oblong of white cloth which knocked the milling muddle of polished black arms and faces round Insel's pallor into a factitious distance, although he and his mates were actually attached to my supper table.

The group being occupied it was difficult to know how to greet them. I swept an inclusive smile of welcome across them as I sat down and the waiter brought the food.

As I watched this virtually prohibited conjunction with a race whose ostracism "debunks" humanity's ostensible belief in its soul, I scarcely heard the scandalous din they were making; these negresses, with their fingers of twig, were tearing at some object—my scarlet packet of "High-Life"!— rapidly becoming invisible under Insel's touch—he clung to it with such constrictive tenacity, he might have been squeezing an atom.

"*Maquereau!*" "*Salaud!*" shrieked the dark ladies to stress their pandemonium accounting of benefits bestowed.

"Insel," I addressed him authoritatively, not dreaming "pimp" and "skunk" were almost the only French words familiar to the poor dear, "if you could understand what they are calling you—you'd let go!"

Once more fallen sideways off himself like his own dead leaf in one of those unexpected carvings into profile; a zig-zag profile of a jumping jack cut out of paper from an exercise book; shrunken to a strip of introvert concentration blind as a nerve among the women's volume, clenching his gums in a fearful sort of constipated fervor, as if hammering on an anvil, Insel thumped his closest negress with an immature fist. Every thump drove in my impression—as this black and white flesh glanced off one another—of their being totally unwed—that Insel, whom I often called "*Ameise*" who was even now like an "ant," occupied with his problem of a load in another dimension, could never have worked on those polished bodies than with the microscopic function of a termite—unseeing, unknowing of all save an imperative to adhere—to never let go. He clung to my cigarettes conscious of nothing but his comic "tic."

There were onlookers peering under the brass rail topping the back-to-back upholstery—three heads left over from the crowded hours. One, the sharp mask of a Jew worn to a rudder with centuries of steering through hostile masses, lowered its pale eyelashes on the neighbors' insurrection as if closing a shop.

I paid the waiter, bought some more cigarettes, jumped into a taxi, undressed and went to bed, all with the delicious composure Insel instilled—not questioning the continuity of this "elevation of the pure in heart" even while he in whom it originated was being slapped by inexpensive harlots on their way home from work.

I was falling into blissful sleep when a hopeless S.O.S. vibrated on the air—an S.O.S. that sounded like a sobbing "*sterben.*" I started up in horror of my selfishness. What could I have been thinking of to leave that delicate soul to his longing for suicide on the contemptible grounds that I was sick of the racket he had been causing.

What would he do, on emerging from a dimension where a packet of ten cigarettes encompassed a universe, to find that I, his very means of expression, had deserted him. With an aereal ease I must have "caught" from Insel, I threw on my clothes and more or less floating into the street together with the presage of dawn, the hoses of the street cleaners slushing my ankles, hounded by my ever growing obsession that Insel held a treasure to be saved at all costs. Damp and heroic I arrived at the Dôme. The piebald mix-up had disappeared.

"What happened to that skeleton I had with me an hour ago?" I asked the majordomo. "He got into a tangle with some negresses— Was he all right?"

"Oh, perfectly," he protested as if within his reach nothing could possibly go wrong. "You see, madame," confidentially, "the fellow lives off these women of the Dôme; there's bound to be a scrap every now and then!"

10

—**ONE** WHO HAS GREATLY suffered," I was astounded to hear myself telling the man—like a nice old maid with illusions—in precisely the somber tones of Insel's "patroness drive." Equally astounded, he shrugged his shoulders.

"You'll find him in one of the little bars round here—he won't be far, madame."

I knew better. I had my own vision of him—it was the rustiness of that nail that haunted me. Or would I reach his attic only after an ebony vampire had sucked the last drop of blood from his corrupted carcass?

Nevertheless, on my swift passage I caught sidelong sight of Insel standing disproportionately at the end of a row of little men before a "zinc," his head, appearing enormous, shone with a muted gleam.

Without stopping I raised my hand. Insel,

although he had his back to me, rushed into the street—he seemed to be continuing to run around.

In his gesture I could see a conclusion of distressful searching in which he had circled during my absence—beating his breast. *"Warum, warum, ist diese Frau davon gegangen?*—Why did this woman go away? I have not ceased to ask myself." Insel complained again and again in miserable bewilderment. "You went away— Why did you go away?"

"Only to fetch something I left at the other cafe."

Tenderly confidential he bent his neck—a gnarl in a stricken tree—I was about to learn what urgent anxiety had drawn me out of bed.

"There was a waiter," he whispered hoarsely into my hat, "who wouldn't let me out of the Dôme until I had paid for two *cafés fines.*" (They had forgotten to include them when I paid for the supper.) "It isn't that I want you to pay me back," he protested with his so distinguished courtesy—."

I always had to order the same drinks for myself as for Insel, or he would not have taken anything— but I made him drink my *fine*. It would, I felt, have superfluous results were I to even sip alcohol in the company of this weirdly intoxicating creature. At the same time in accordance with my mission as a lifesaver, I begged him to take *café au lait*—which roused a piteous opposition.

As if wound up he went on beating a *mea culpa* on his absent breast.

I caught him by the arm.

Instantaneously he displaced to a distance. I was left with my own arm articulated at a right angle, holding in my hand a few inches of gray bone. It had come away with a bit of his sleeve, acutely decorated with the jagged edge of torn black cloth. At the same time, Insel laying his hand on my shoulder, the rag and the bone did a "fade-out."

"Promise me to stay here," he whispered, "while I go to the bar. These people would not like it if I did not pay."

Insel, who seemed to remember our pact, wanted to go back to the Dôme. But I refused.

"It's time for you to sleep," I commanded. That persistent teeter in my mind which was always tipping Insel up in a stiff horizontal straight line, his immovable eyes glued to infinity, was laying him out in state on no bed under an awesome canopy of poverty.

"No," I decided, "I shall put you back in your box—my pet clochard is going to lie in a row—under a bridge."

11

WE **WANDERED OFF** in search of the Seine— It was dawn.

Perhaps this showcase hung outside a *librairie* was a prison and we, therefore, suspecting an isolation, dissolved its wire caging with the crafty focus of sight to set the content free.

We saw the primeval steam (whose last wisp straying endlessly had wreathed itself round Insel's brain) condense to stone in a frayed torso.

In the darkness it was blind. As the sky broke open, its outline entered the morning gently with the eyes of an animal. As daylight warmed the lids widened to the vision of a pagan.

In conception vast enough to absorb the centuries it survived, now in defiance of time to surpass it—the eternal Thing was looking at us with the fullness of the future. All we had ever understood that was less than itself peeled like spoiled armor.

What enormous foreboding, Insel, in his simplicity, I, in my complexity, recognized in its ideal expression, I cannot say. It was a recognition of something known which, in spite of life, we would know again. Insel, without speaking, turned to me staring at the re-impression of an impression on a book spread out for the passerby we had both, I could see, in identical silence found one significance in an early Greek fragment—I do not remember which.

I have heard that some philosophers assume reality to be absent without an audience. In empty streets the sun had a terrible excessive existence for ourselves alone. We walked together, yet repeatedly, as if having veered in an arc it took no time to describe, Insel would be coming towards me from far away.

"Go back!" he cried in gaunt derangement, "if it disgusts you to look at me." Shining uselessly, as an electric bulb "left on" by day, his face, unshaven, was partially clouded.

We came to a Raoul Dufy in a dealer's window; his charming "crook's technique" disintegrated my meticulous companion. I feared that, the shock reinforcing his perpetual cerebral fit, he was about to throw a physical one. Instead he became covered with verdigris.

We had to relapse at another cafe. Insel disappeared for quite a while.

"Have you been sick?" I asked solicitously. He was looking less green.

"Dufy," he explained.

I put down the money for the coffee and a twenty-five centime piece rolled to the ground.

"Would you pick that up?" I begged. Insel began pulling himself together but did nothing about it, so I picked it up myself.

"Oh, dear," he wailed forlornly. "I thought you pointed to me. For God's sake throw it down again—or I shall never forgive myself," he pled and pled—.

Nothing would induce me to. I foresaw him distinctly diminishing through the hole in the center of that tiny disc and I had to get him to the Seine.

At length we arrived at the gleaming water bearing so lightly its lazy barges with their drag of dancing diamonds. Whatever had been an "under-the-bridge" was all boxed in and the sun had crawled so far into the sky it was needless to look for another.

After that we seemed to be wandering in an aimless delight round and round the Orangerie. Insel's boots were hurting. His pain was impersonal; it might have been following him, snapping at his legs.

With some effort, having breakfasted all night, we conceived the idea of going to "lunch." Insel, who was on the point of allowing the air to lift him from the railed-in terrace of the Tuileries and set him down in the Rue de la Paix, appraised by normal standards, although it was just this "beauty of horror" I was sure should be worth such a lot of money to him, looked really terrifying. His being unshaven became a smoke screen. Always his self-illumination cast its own shadow. In shining he dragged an individual darkness into the world. I felt sure that as the thoroughfares refilled we would run less risk of being arrested for disturbing the public peace on the Left Bank.

"My friend we are not dressed for going into town," I insisted, heading him off in another direction.

"Why?" asked Insel in bewildered politeness. "You look as lovely as you always do."

With a bizarre instinct for scenic effect the hazard presiding our senseless excursion drove us into the Gare d'Orléans.

In the almost gelatinous gloom of the great hall the enclosure before the Buffet Restaurant, its boundaries set by stifled shrubs, offered a stage for Insel to unroll his increate existence to the fitting applause of a dead echo, the countless scurry of departing feet.

This station, as he entered it, became the anteroom of dissolution, where the only constructions left of a real world were avalanches of newspapers, and even these aligned in a dusty perspective like ghosts of overgrown toys.

The place seemed deserted. There was no one to see Insel lay out hocus-pocus negresses on the table in apologetic sacrifice.

"They were *all wrong*," he brooded, as if he were a puritan with an ailing conscience. "I was going in the wrong direction!— I renounce," he sobbed hurling off the negresses, who, bashed against the dingy windows of the Gare, melted and dripped like black tears into limbo down a morbid adit leading to underground platforms—there to mingle with the inquietude of departure to be borne away on a hearse of the living throbbing along an iron rail which must be a solidified sweep of the Styx.

"The only thing wrong with those negresses was your beating one of them up!"

Insel denied this vehemently, and reproached me. I had, he said, inflamed their rebellion by smiling at them. That was no way to handle negresses.

"What? You can sleep with them, but I can't smile at them. How do you work that out?"

This muddled Insel, the theme of whose half-conscious theatricals must either be that his beefsteak shared jealous passions with less conclusively slaughtered meat or that prostitutes lay far beyond a patroness's permissions.

"Colored people are not—," he began, looking very Simon Legree.

"But Insel in your relationship she is entitled—"

"I only slept with her three times—"

"If she had slept with you *half a time* I consider she has a right to everything you possess."

Insel, who had a fanciful ingenuity in extricating himself from any situation he felt to be awkward without very well understanding why, instructed me, "You know nothing of the etiquette of *my* underworld—its *laws*. The rights of such women extend only to the level of the tabletop.

"It's like this—I am sitting at the Dôme—she comes along—"

"She dropped on you," I corrected— It was fun

teasing him. Like tickling a dazed gnome with a spider's silk.

Ignoring my interruption, he continued, "She may take *anything* under the table—she can grab a thousand francs from my pocket—it is hers. But to lift anything *off* the table—*ausgeschlossen!*—impermissible!"

So exactly the logic on behalf of woman in the normal world that I squeaked, "You haven't got a thousand francs in your pocket."

What matter if we were trivial. We must find some excuse for our unending hazy laughter. Speech was an afterthought to that humorous peace as it fused with our incomparable exaltation. It was ridiculous to find ourselves, alone, in well-being so wide there was room for innumerable populations.

Insel harped back to *not* having beaten the negress.

"Well," I temporized, relenting, "you thumped her— You did like this," clinching every nerve in my body I tried to imitate that excruciation which in him took the place of a sense of touch— But my fingers closed on an absence—incipience of all volume, Insel's volume. "Didn't you know?"

All he could remember was her stealing my cigarettes.

"Stealing," I exclaimed, "the waiter told me they support you—."

"Everybody," Insel reflected drearily, "thinks I am such an awful *maquereau*. I only had three meals with them."

"You don't have to exonerate yourself," I said dryly, overcome with compassion. "It's quite a feat—being a pimp and starving to death." Then laughing, "Whoever heard of a *maquereau* without any money!" It made such a gorgeous sound when they were shouting—almost *macrusallo*. Like crucified mackerel—

"They stole my sheets," Insel interrupted sternly, "my six white sheets."

"Six sheets against three meals or three embraces! Whichever way you put it your honor is clear," I consoled him, "All the same, I shall not call you *clochard* any more, but *macrusallo*."

Insel's luminous duality peculiar to this one night seemed to be forming a more domestic hallucination, an elfin attempt at flirtation, miraculously coy, which played all to itself against the greater glow and measure of his basic disarray—a tacit assumption of our having mutually renounced an inferior world in spite of his repulsiveness being, as he wailed, greater than I could bear.

I had once, to get a simple opinion, asked my dressmaker to take a look at him.

"Well, do you think he's mad?" I asked her.

"He looks so funny," she giggled. "He looks 'in love.' "

She was right, he had the air of being amorous of anything or everything in general which left him so rapt and gentle, or, taking an "inner" view, his astral Venus flowed in his veins. This was why, when he met a woman, Mme Feirlein or any other, he had an approach of continent rape, as if he were persuading her bemused, "See! It must be the more lovely for being already consummate."

For a moment I wondered if his unstaid mind had reconceived in some unguessable aspect I assumed for him, its eerie durable passion in general—for myself. But apart from the likelihood of his having no idea as to whom he alternately bewailed and beamed upon, I remembered the only emotion I aroused in creative men was an impulse of "knock-out" (that any intuited opposition of the future stirs in the subconscious) which of course was *impossible* with this delicate soul swimming so docilely along his astral stream under the thunder and lightnings of his distraction like a confiding duck as I scattered crumbs.

At the same time a worn down record of old-fashioned inflection clattered out of Insel's head:

"In spite of all—"

A lesson? A suggestion? A refrain to be taken up?

Instantly I knew this to be a touch-word on which some spring must snap, some wheel fly wild. That, as I watched, something horrible, in anguish, was *wanting to happen*—a dangerous inertia waiting to be acted upon by some external irritant.

Our lake of peace was draining as Insel gathered himself together for some voluntary magnetic onslaught "in spite of all" had swollen on the air—

Shafts from his eyes became so penetrating I could feel myself dissolve to a transparent target, they pierced me, and, travelling to the further side, stared through my back on their return to his irises.

He seemed to collect electricity from the air (in the afternoon there was a violent storm). This crackling electricity flashed so nearby without attaining to me. It was as if I were *almost* leaning up against a lightning conductor. I remembered his girl's watch was still in my handbag—it lay beside me—a kind of self-focus in his magnetic field.

He had always something about him of a lithe tree struck by its own lightning.

These magnetic tides would rise and ebb as we sat in felicity around an enormous *plat anglais,* which I could not touch for my absorption in Insel and of which, as Insel ate of it, the rosy meats seemed to drop uselessly into void. And all the while Insel spasmodically kept up his bum's charade pleading for variable salvations. With his floppy pathos he implored me to take pity on him, to take him in—I would see how I would work with Insel keeping house for me with that precision he exercised in his own dimension—to put him in a nursing home and surround him with angelic choirs of pretty nurses "only to look at," he exclaimed—persuasive or timorous.

I had seen the actor Moisse by the light of a little candle remember some human tie in a prison cell; the humble flame drawing him into itself spread his reminiscent spirit over the callous walls to warm them. Such a candle was burning behind Insel's eyes as if he were his own narrow room. Yet the lines of its rays shining to infinite remoteness—a state of consciousness closing out the world—laid their ethereal carpets along the ceaseless levels of annihilation.

No rock, no root, no accident of Nature varied a virgin plain that had conceived no landscape, and I saw Insel reduced to the proportion he would have in the eye of a God—setting out—unaccompanied, unorientated, for here where nothing existed, no sound, no sun, reigned an unimaginable atmosphere he longed to breathe. I could see this, because he was seeing this, as still hanging back, he writhed to its lure. Although I promised solicitously to send him to a nursing home, we knew I could not come to his aid—. He had never told me *where he was.* His torment tantalized pity.

With that acrobatic facility he had for immeasurable leaps from despair to cajolery—he readjusted himself to the station buffet—as if to get down to some business.

12

HIS EYES NOW PACIFIED in a steady human mesmerism smiled cosily into mine.

"*An was denken Sie?*" he asked in coquettish

anticipation. "What are you thinking of?" Again I had that creepy impression of ultimate tension, of a cerebral elastic taut for the snap.

"—of you," wheezed the battered record turning on his brain to my sudden visualization of Insel as a gray tomcat having a fit in a cloud of ashes and lunar spangles.

I could not tell him, no thought coincided between one on the verge of dwelling among the levels he laid bare to me and one who remained outside.

Still he went on smiling a little vaingloriously. "*An was denken Sie?*" he asked again, of God knows what girl, in God knows what decade, and all the same of me.

In my veritable séances with Insel, the clock alone retrieved me from nonentity—thrusting its real face into mine as reminder of the temporal.

Thus I saw how three whole hours went by while Insel asked me what I was thinking of. They passed off in a puff as though, for a change, he had contracted time into intensity.

All the whimsical nonsense ever conceived rotated on his eyeballs which seemed to convey "while I pretend to search for some secret in you the less danger is there of your being inquisitive as to mine."

With every question his eyes grew greater, thrust out longer spears, unctuous in the aromatic ooze from his brain.

"What are you thinking of?" urged Insel, and the

softer fell his voice, the more inflexible he knit himself together—the more terrifically to disintegrate on some signal he invoked.

So I sat with as soothing and expressionless a smile as I could concoct and answered occasionally, "I am thinking of June 18th, 1931, or of 9 o'clock on Tuesday of the week before last. —What are you thinking of?" His eyes converging on me, a yellow glow fused to a single planetary dilation rapped on the sun gong. "—*An was denken Sie?*" Insel, discouraged, petrified his face before me—with a determination beyond all human power, in the "last expression" that death imposes on pain. Incredibly exact, rivalling even any original I had seen.

"I should have preferred," he said with his voice of dead lovers crying through the earth, "to be fit for you to look at." Then he deliberately set himself on fire.

In exact description—he did not consistently appear to the naked eye, as a bonfire, in a normal degree of comparison to the morning murk sifting through the glassed environment. As a thread in the general mass, he retained his depth of tone. But as if his astounding vibratory flux required a more delicate instrument than the eye for registration. Some infrared or there invisible ray he gave off, was immediately transferred on one's neural current to some dark room in the brain for instantaneous development in all its brilliancy. So one saw him as a gray man and an electrified organism at one and the same time—

—it was only the candle spluttering . . . preliminary to the most beautiful spectacle I have ever "seen."

Shaken with an unearthly anxiety, this creature of so divine a degradation, set upon himself with his queer hands and began to pull off his face.

For those whose flesh is their rags, it is not pitiable to undress.

As Insel dropped the scabs of his peculiar astral carbonization upon the table, his cheeks torn down, in bits upon the marble—one rift ran the whole length of his imperfect insulation, and for a moment exposed the "man-of-light."

He sat there inside him taking no notice at all, made of the first jelly quivering under the sun and some final unimaginable form of aereal substance, in the same eternal conviction as the Greek fragment—

Once at dark in the Maine woods, I had stumbled on a rotten log. The scabs of foetid bark flew off revealing a solid cellulose jewel. It glowed in the tremendous tepidity of phosphorescence from a store of moonlight similar to condensed sun in living vegetables.

At last Insel's eyes dying of hallucination, stared suddenly into the filtered day. Horrified almost to blindness he complained, "*Es ist zu hell.*" He sounded as if deliberately quoting "it is too light"— That did not matter after all the ways he had been "happening."

"So you're starving, are you?" I mocked,

exasperated with his total inability to estimate himself. "The greatest actor alive."

As I took him out, Insel suddenly blew hundreds of yards ahead. He was pirouetting perplexedly around himself when I caught up with him and we got into a cab.

In that small space he behaved like a fish on the end of a line, like a kite in the air entangled in its own tail—carrying about with him, in his awful unrest, my hand to which he clung—his own had clamped so fast to it, he could hardly get it off—when I dropped him at his door.

13

I WAS READY TO LEAVE for Saint-Cloud with

my little valise when there came a soft knocking on the door I was about to open, a knocking irreal as the fall of dusk. Insel had turned up again. He collapsed before me like a stricken gull having received some unavowable hurt in the unknown wastes where he belonged. The storm must have completely disintegrated his exceptional electrification.

"*Um Gottes Willen,*" he panted almost inaudibly. "I cannot eat, I cannot sleep, and now my heart is ceasing to beat."

It was remarkable he should succeed in speaking—his body no longer showed much sign of life. He might be using this body—with its interwoven identity of the living remains of a dead man and the dead remains of a man once alive—as a medium, from a distance to which his fluctuant spirit had been temporarily released.

His face having lost its bruised appearance was set in the tidy waxen consistency that makes corpses look like sudden dolls.

I might be entertaining a ghost, so light a labor I found it to draw him through the glass doors into the studio. As I dropped him onto an enormous couch, my everyday self broadcast a panic.

"Mrs. Jones, her daughter having sailed for New York, is discovered alone in her flat with a dead tramp."

Briefly I thought of *blowing* the thing out of the window. The seeming imminence of his death allowed for no other means of getting rid of him. But this was no solution. He would be found—sprawled in the courtyard.

Then it came to me that in spite of my willful descent into a forbidden psychology, I still had sufficient power to put him to rest. "Insel," I inquired, "can you hear me?" Then—very slowly—very distinctly, "You are going to sleep—sleep till the blue moon."

There surged out of Insel a whisper of horror, "But my heart isn't beating," he protested.

"That is only a neurotic illusion," I consoled him, believing I lied.

He lay on the couch and did not die. I began to arrange for a possible revival. "Is there anything you can drink that isn't alcoholic?" I asked him quietly.

After a while he murmured, "*Pfeffermintztee.*"

"Try to be alive when I come back," I urged him in all sincerity.

"Where are you going?" he wanted to know, his voice a hoarse agony.

"To buy *pfeffermintztee.*"

"No—no—you're not to leave me—*ever.*"

With a strange grip of a limp vice his fingers clung to my wrist. I had to sit down beside him. Now he was staring as if bewitched, at the parquet of the floor.

"The peppermint won't grow out of the floor," I advised.

"It will," said Insel. "You're to stay here."

And I found myself staring together with him.

It was no peppermint growing out of the planes of polished oak. Only the creeping organic development of a microscopic undergrowth such as carpeted chaos in his work, almost as closely cramped as the creamy convolutions of a brain. Foliage of mildew it spread—and spread.

"An infusion of that fungus would be bad for you," I persuaded him, taking his fingers carefully apart, lifting their tentacular pulp from my wrist.

Escaping I rushed to the shop at the corner and

back again. As Insel was still living, I made him his tea.

"And you will be able to sleep," he reproached me, oblivious of his drowsiness as he fell asleep.

I could watch over my invalid through a pane of glass incompletely covered by a curtain on the door at the far end of the studio.

A dense oppression stole through the flat all packed up in its iron shutters. Insel, who had no longer been able to bear a light, lay pallid and obscure in a faint reflection from a lantern in the hall, his slumber the extinction of a dim volcano. Lax as a larva, a glow worm "gone out," his head bared of its phosphorescent halo, seemed swollen in a meaningless hydrocephalus. As if, while conscious, electric emissions had diminished his cranial volume.

Around him the atmosphere was stale as an alcohol preserving a foetal monster he resembled in repose.

Insel was unpleasant bereft of his radiance.

His body had dwindled in distilling an immaterial essence to such concentration it was appreciable to the senses. One was aware of an effulgence, which, if it waxed and waned during his waking hours, had now altogether vanished. His body swept and garnished like the house in the Bible—devilishly invaded—was no longer human as it lay before me in the form of Insel.

There unshining and supine he seemed abandoned of all quality except the opaque. The gray inflated opacity of his unseeing head, which, should one lift it from the pillow, must surely loll on his shoulder—the head of an idiot.

The flat seemed emptier for his being there, until I found that further off it was filled to a weird expansion with emanations drifting away from Insel asleep. They crowded the air, minute horizontal icicles, with a tingling of frozen fire. In the room at the end of the corridor their force of vitalized nothingness was pushing back the walls. Why should Insel, less ponderable than other men, impart perceptible properties to the Air? Was he leaking out of himself, residuum of that ominous honey he stored behind his eyes into which it was his constant, his distraught concern to withdraw?

In his soaring, flagging excitations he might have spent a spiritual capital and going broke, be raising exhaustive loans on the steadily decreasing collateral of his vitality, until an ultimate bonfire in those eerie eyes should be extinguished in some unimaginable bankruptcy.

In him the intangible and tangible components of a human being had come apart. As if in some ruthless extraction of Supreme Good from a fallible pulp, the vibrancy interpenetrating normal muscular fiber had been indrawn from his physical structure to condense in a point of flame. When some mysterious fuel failed him, Insel remained—a mess of profane dross.

I thought of his pictures, those queerly luminous almost materializing projections. Curious creatures moving in levitation—frequently cerebral abortions of cats.

Any student of ancient occultism would recognize them for elementals. Imbecilic, vampiric—here and there an obsessive absence of a mouth implied an inconceivable constipation. A conspicuous liver, so personal he might have served as his own fluoroscope, clear as a pale coral was painted as only the Masters painted. He had no need to portray. His pictures grew, out of him, seeding through the inter-atomic spaces in his digital substance to urge tenacious roots into a plane surface.

I wondered in what psychic succession these monsters issued from a man, who himself when unlit or cut into profile, became so hauntingly animal, even insectile. Who, when asleep, being the makings of his own bestiary, was vilely void as an incubus—wondered why millenary monsters of a disreputable metaphysic should re-arise intact in a modern subconscious.

Insel slept for twenty hours. With one interruption. When I went in to see how he was I woke him up.

Through the slits in the shutters the outdoor lights laid narrow blades along the floor, above Insel's feet on the whitewashed wall they crossed and cast a double shadow of a hanging fern. Otherwise the room was a mausoleum.

Again I could have sworn I beheld the dead. Silence had hardened upon him in a stony armor, too heavy for the fluttering of breath.

I listened till the sound of his rigidity grew so shrill I was forced to make it mute. Terrified, I took hold of the door and crashed it to.

Insel—who after all must, of his nature, float quite lightly on the surface of a coma—easily lifted his lids.

"I'm sorry to have disturbed you," I gasped. "It was necessary to make a noise to know you are not dead."

With none of the daze of sudden rousing he excused me gently. And slept anew.

Those depths through which others plunge into sleep for him stretched shallow as moisture on a mirror.

In the morning I went out, off into the sunlight, shopping. Leaving far behind me that darkened room, and whatever it contained.

My major purchase was kilos of bright red beef.

When he awoke I fed him chunks from a great frying pan. Insel sat up and swallowed them with fairly bestial satisfaction.

"Why," I asked to make conversation, "do you always want 'Fleisch ohne Knochen'?"

I had taken it for granted he ordered boneless meat to avoid waste. But Insel began peering about shockingly as if suspicious of being overheard.

"When I am alone," he explained, in an unexpectedly vacuous voice, "I do not eat like this—I have to drag bones into a corner—to gnaw."

I felt curious to know how—without teeth—. But Insel beginning to shine again put off the animal, to become the clown of an angel.

Through the row of glass doors the ornaments in the hall looked like fish under water as a celadon tide of pale lamplight sluiced into the studio. From the shutters on either side, entangled reflections flickered into the halo that was now re-forming round Insel's face.

Stark on the *sommier* he floated up from the floor of a pool with the wavering fungus he had sown there clinging to his cover.

He told me he had found the secret of perpetual motion if only he had the money to buy the stuff. To me it seemed he had rather discovered a slow time that must result in eternity.

I told him I had for some while been conceiving a ballet.

"It is the story of a maiden seeing her life in a crystal— It would look exactly as it does here, everything translucent." I waved to Insel—"Yet as in the days when there were maidens they had no 'life,' what she sees is her future spouse sowing his 'wild oats.'

"All dancers are terribly ponderable after Nijinsky—yet once I came across one who possessed a dual *equipoise* which threw him into a huddle with himself. That is how my youth would dance, with the wild oats springing up to the moon around him, whichever way he turned— But I should have to do maquettes—animated maquettes of the choreography—and *I* can't make *anything* grow out of the floor," I said deferentially.

"Of course he makes love to everything. A

cocotte's eye. The woman in the litmus petticoat forecasting the weather. A rainbow," I continued, seeing Insel entranced. "The Queen of Fairyland—Mermaids and Medusae." Envy was stealing into Insel.

"I dance divinely," he said and I could see him crossing a ballroom floor propelled as if on invisible casters, as truly initiate acolytes, in reception and remittance of the Holy Book before the high altar.

"Always at the crucial moment the youth is intercepted. There comes floating in between him and the object of his concupiscence, a—" I stopped, as Insel, seemingly relieved by the frustration of a rival, closed his eyes, and waited till he came to. "Over and again I drop the idea in despair. Over and over again I find a solution so simple it constantly slips my mind. I have only to make some little people about five inches high and tell them what to dance." Insel nodded comprehendingly. "Yet whenever I get to work I come upon some fundamental obstacle. It takes me *hours*," I complained to Insel, "to remember it cannot be done. It is as if at the back of that memory stands another memory of having had the power to create whatever I pleased."

Insel's eyes enlarged in a ruminative stare. The stealthy oncreep of his visual lichen had reached the walls. We had no longer need of larynxes to converse. Insel *thought at me*. More precisely—vaguely conceived before me.

"To make things grow," he conveyed on his silence, "you would have to begin with the invisible dynamo of growth; it has the dimension of naught and the Power of Nature. As a rule it will only grow if planted in a woman— But *my brain* is a more exquisite manure. In that time in which I exist alone, I recover the Oceanic grain of life to let it run through my fingers, multiple as sand."

Then the silence of Insel took on voice once more— A voice which as if returning from diffusion among the mists—might be coming from "anywhere," resumed his ever recurrent cries of horror on behalf of women who could no longer love him.

"For God's sake," I implored, for Insel returned to his "normal" state, I followed suit—"stop agonizing— Go to sleep— To negresses *every* white man looks—white."

"It's the teeth," he groaned—"*Die Mädchen—*"

At least you'd have more chance with the girls if you got Bebelle to clean your suit—

"I'll tell you what," I said, overcome by my inherent conviction of personal blame for *anyone* not being able to get *anything* they want—. And in Insel it seemed his need was for something so sublime that over all his aspirations hovered crowns of glory—*Mädchen*—something entirely outside my zone of attraction, in his regret for them, took on enchanting attributes—even those in a mountain village who ate such quantities of garlic it breathed from the pores of their skin—so much so that Insel, with the heartiest will in the world, had found it impossible to "hug them close enough."

"You'd better get *into* that couch and leave your suit in the hall—when I come home I'll throw it into a bath of gasoline."

Insel was horrified. "I don't want anybody to see the dirt in that suit—let alone you—I've worn it for five years."

"All I shall see is the gasoline go dark—it would seem just as dark if I were cleaning something that had only been worn six months."

But Insel was actually writhing in a bitter determination to protect his own.

"Are you afraid," I asked, in a sudden concern for his "rays," "that it would interfere with your *Strahlen*?—I'm not going to wash it. You can't short-circuit."

On the contrary—I anticipated him distinctly renewed in an intenser radiance—

"Please," I begged—enraptured as a nun seeking permission to lay fresh lilies before a shrine. "*Ich bitte Sie.*"

He was obdurate—it would seem, in shame. It did not occur to me that in cleaning him up one would be cutting a slice from his "beggar's capital."

"It's not distinguished to be ashamed—"

Insel, in a way, gave in—.

"You try it," he warned me. "Before your eyes the suit will turn white."

"It won't, or if it does, I'll turn it black again."

"You may clean it forever," he intoned

ominously—"the while it grows whiter—and whiter."

"*Mädchen,*" I reminded him for bait—"or at least," as for an instant Insel's ravaged features showed through his ennobling aura—"better negresses."

Insel was pacified. But he did not go to sleep. He evaporated.

I recognized a vapor whose drifting suspension of invisible myriads he copied so passionately with the overfine point of his pencil.

When it cleared off it had left him again an effigy straightened as the level of water.

The world of the Lutetia had materialized. An infiltration of half-light softly bursting the dark, a thin cascade, the ferns dripping into a green gloom. Here, where dawn and noon and midnight were all so dim and Insel lay sensitive to clarity as a creature of the deep sea; the closely shuttered studio with its row of glass doors was a real replica of the irreal "aquarium."

Because I found the place somewhat chilly when sunless—I had thrown a great white blanket over my thin dress. This was due to no obsession for Insel's white miracles. Simply, everything being put away in naphthalene, this had returned from the cleaners and the *femme de ménage* had not yet locked it up.

Fairly inflexible—it curved around me loosely, encaving me—its stiff corner trailing off like a sail.

I sat on the edge of the couch at the feet of that rigid flotsam—in a huge white shell.

Again I received a strictly lateral invitation to wholly exist in a region imposing a supine inhabitance. A region whose architecture, being parallel to Paradise, is only visible to a horizontal gaze. Should one stand up to it, it must disappear.

Somehow, unable to dissolve into mist, and thus too dense to enter a mirage, the nearest I could conform to the arid aquatic was in becoming crustacean.

Being an outsider did not interfere with my participation in the ebullient calm behind Insel's eyelids, where cerebral rays of imprecision, lengthening across an area of perfectibility, were intercepted by resonant images audible to the eye, visible to the ear; where even ultimate distance was brought within reach, tangible as a caress.

As all this "lasted forever" it seemed incompatible that Insel should slump back into a larva. Yet there he was—extinguished again in unregenerative sleep.

I turned to go. A scatter of objects on the table attracted my attention. Among some weary sous and tiny strangulated worms—broken shoe laces—lay evidently the bone of some prehistoric fish. A white comb shrill with the accumulated phosphorus of the ages. Insel had emptied out his pockets.

I went about my cleaning. Ordering several *bidons* of gasoline, I poured them into an enamel tub, and suspending the suit by a wooden pincers, I dipped it in.

The sun was shining, the kitchen blazing white.

Before the open windows that which seemed most substantial about Insel, like a corpse let down from a gallows, fell to its knees in the volatile fluid.

Then the ghastly thing began to turn pale. I set upon it in opposition and that white contorted outgrowth of a brain almost tangled in the whisk-brush—.

Had he really intended as much in his challenge—or did this Polar region of a mania— these maps of Himalayan anthills with their scabs of pure vegetation embossed upon the backdrop of his clothes, depend for their pictorial clarity on some accord between his cerebral vibrations and mine?

Being tired and bored, I went in to see if in exchange for some more food, I could make terms with Insel.

He appeared uneasy. Rolling his eyes like runaway wheels spoked with interrogations. His expression was such as I had never seen. Terror solidified.

"I am a prisoner here!"

It did not recur to me that his classic complaint is an echo in the corridors of asylums.

Tearing my visionary trappings of meat and such from me with his flippant accusation, Insel did not at all want to know, "When shall I see you again?"— He had never seen me before.

My everyday self shuddered—"Blackmail! Almost as awkward as dead tramps." I reflected, but I had become so nicely attuned to Insel's moods that my parasitic clairvoyance, of its very nature, being constrained to see eye to eye with him, immediately veered to his viewpoint, I concluded I must in a temporary aberration have kidnapped this gaunt guest whose snarl was unsociable.

"Beefsteak," I quavered, as if enticing a surly hound.

Insel, completely jammed between infinite walls, was not having any steak.

I must dislodge his attention.

Seemingly at hazard my dilemma linked up with one of the kind of infantile anecdotes Insel always greeted with glee.

"Have you heard about the Hungarian immigrant lost in London?" I inquired as engagingly as I could. "He wanted to find his consulate and could not understand why the policeman only shrugged his shoulders when he explained he was 'Hungry.' "

Strange how unerringly the unconscious picks its way. I had "found" Insel for himself again. To the Titan of Hunger—the policeman's shoulders heaved in the shrug of all humanity ignoring Insel. This recognition shook him with the most sophisticated laughter I have ever heard in my life.

"Your suit has turned white," I announced.

A gleam of crafty assurance stole into his transparent eyes.

"You will never 'get out' while your suit is white," I threatened, "all die Mädchen are on the other side of the wall—"

"Oh," said Insel with a conciliatory smile, "I only want them to look at."

"Well, they won't look at you until your suit is black; and as we're about it you'd better let me clean your shirt."

His shirt was of a dark gray design rather mellow. When I suggested renovation he clutched it by the open throat.

"See," he said, lifting it with a cautious yet ostentatiously offhand gesture, "the neckband is worn ragged inside—it's not worth it." He was cowering in some apprehension that constricted him, that even devitalized his hand. Become as the hand of a victim of infantile paralysis, it flopped over with the edge of the stuff. He had an air of shifting—just so far—the bandage of a wound.

Not for the first time, with Insel, I received a subliminal flash of an apostate Saint Sebastian writhing with arrows—in such privacy, it would be indelicate to intrude upon it with whatever assistance.

On looking back, it seems inconsistent, that once the elation he inspired in me died down—I should have continued in my obsession of conserving something very precious with an Insel changing to an incubus, playing his silly psychic tricks on his clothes—raving of imprisonment and the gnawing of *Knochen*. It had left me with the solicitude one might have for a valued friend with whom one has been on some glorious drinking bout, when he shows up next day at a disadvantage in a particularly nasty hangover.

One last struggle with the suit—and it turned black again. Insel must have forgotten about it.

14

"BREAKFAST," I announced.

This time Insel did not stir.

His head, although returned to normal volume scarcely indented the pillow. He was set in the perfect quadrates of a couch, having no rumple anywhere. As he lay upon it without taking contact with it, the comfortable bulges of covers tucked under a mattress sharpened to corners of trigonometric exactitude.

The smoothing systemizing vibrations that straightened his surroundings, obviously did not issue from his frame, which had half-died for contributing vitality to some focus of force.

Perhaps they were transmitted by his hair. I have always presumed that hair with its electric properties will not remain unutilized in a future evolution of the brain.

His hair—what little was left—was so fine, that without amalgamating, it had the unity of surface of the horny plate with which hair furnishes the extremities in its aggregate form of a nail.

Tentatively—I touched that hair, repeating "Breakfast" on a cheerful note—to appear as if I were patting his head to wake him up.

In a decreased microscopic degree, my fingers encountered the same onslaught as had my whole person in the corridor. A sharp crackle of inconceivably minuscule machine guns carried to some psychic center of my ear.

The effect was astonishing as when I had tapped him on the arm. Insel did not awaken—he turned his head as if he were pushing it up into strata of delight above him. Which on contact melted upon his face in a slow smile.

He was smiling as if the tip of the wing of an angel had fanned him.

Again, as I watched, I had the sensation of "breaking point," an expectance of a spring flying loose to whirr insanely.

His face, like stale bread smeared with his private honey, stood still.

Then it broke.

With the unforeseen ugliness opening up suddenly emerging hippopotami *the gums* in their hideous defenselessness *observed* me—an obscene enjoyment of ill-will pleated his clamped lids.

His teeth had not decayed. They were *worn* down.

Der Totenkopf hung in my tract of vision like the last of *Alice in Wonderland*'s Cheshire cat.

Getting in touch with Insel was the whole itinerary of Good and Evil.

In the passing away of a miasma Insel awakened. Although never much the better for food, his temperament having relieved itself of some disproportionate impulse in that monomaniac gape, he now seemed normalized.

It was a serene creature who began to breakfast. Whatever introspective conflict usually engaged him, it had ceased.

"You really look rather well now. Why don't you just stay and have that rest cure *here*. I'll hire Bebelle to feed you—do everything for you while you lie down and drowse till you're quite fit. I *must* get back to Saint-Cloud."

"Impossible," moaned Insel, instantly sagging, "I have to return to my troubles. You do not understand. They are my life. It waits for me."

"Nonsense, you spent the night in Montparnasse in one incessant gurgle of laughter."

"It was a *hollow* laughter," he intercepted, sepulchrally. Insel had resumed his "line" which seemed so inadequate.

Should I risk an attempt to reveal to Insel those real-essences in Insel? Real-essences to a slight degree rationalized for my mind, they might be either the very symptoms of the so-called madness in him, or precisely the incognizable cause of his befuddlement.

"Insel," I set out determinedly. "You must get over your ugliness—it's an obsession! That's not all there is to you—you have some intrinsic quality I have never found in anyone else. It's difficult to tell you about it because I have no idea what it is. But it's something so valuable it's one's duty to keep you alive to discover its nature."

"Several alienists have offered to examine me—regularly—" said Insel, with self-complacence, "twice a week!"

"It's not pathological—only unprecedented. A kind of radio-activity you give off—. Insel," I asked puzzled, "how does the world look to you? Like an Aquarium?"

Insel looking no less puzzled than myself, I was taken aback. But I went on in the hope of striking common ground.

"It was the evening outside the Lutetia I experienced its effects. A sort of doubling of space where different selves lived different ways in different dimensions at once. Sitting on the sidewalk—floating in an Atlantic Ocean full of skyscrapers and ethereal cars. That was not particularly important—the wonder was the sense of timeless peace—of perfect happiness—"

15

INSEL SAT BOLT UPRIGHT in his couch and let out a thin screech like a mad cat; looking exactly as if he had caught a mouse he had watched for a long time.

"No." He wagged his poor bald head judiciously, "*It cannot be*—I can only love forever."

I gave one gasp—then as always when taken unawares, my mother reproved me from my subconscious—a sophisticated middle-aged woman making immodest impressions on an innocent *Schlosser's* son.

"You misunderstand. I had thought of you as a 'Will-o'-the-Wisp.' "

Insel took no heed, he was practically licking his chops.

Quite as if it were an impulse habitual to me, I decided to slug him.

Then he began moaning again—of suffering, which one moment, he could allow me to share, and another, he refused to cause me.

"It would be too fearful for you—the Parting," he pointed out. "You see," he confided affectionately as if promising me a present, "I am going to get her back—"

A spiral craftiness wormed into his eyes as I asked, "Where is she?"

"In South Africa," he answered with some impatience, as if I should have remembered.

This girl in her role of "only beloved" was almost as unsettled as Insel himself. Only yesterday she lived with her Lesbian in Berlin—and now, "Since she left me she has married twice and borne four children." Before very long she actually split in two—

"*Es war eine Schwartze und eine Blonde—*"

"When was she black and blond?" I exclaimed, intrigued.

"Last night, outside the Select—I saw at once they had fallen for me," said Insel, ignoring he had been fast asleep.

"But Insel," I laughed, "can't you remember how terribly miserable you are because you frighten the women?"

"All that is changed now," said Insel looking me over with sadistic compassion.

Quite forgetting my determination to slug him—I glowed with the satisfaction of a successful psychiatrist—"I have cured him of his fixed idea—" I congratulated myself—

Then with his lightning variability of mood, his eyes diluting in a difficult introspection,

"Outside the Lutetia," he pondered wonderingly. "That's funny. I had *exactly* the same experience."

"You couldn't," I was about to retort, "it's not in

Kafka," but checked myself, wishing to keep him on the subject of his radiation.

"That's why I adore talking to you—why I cannot allow you to suffer for me. I know too well what suffering is,"—and suddenly he threw up his head. The almost mummified chords of his throat vibrating in an ecstasy.

"*Die Liebe—wie schön—wie sch-ööö-n—*Love— the one beauty of Life." He gloated with the same singing inflection with which he had been wont to celebrate steak. There *is* nothing else, he concluded. Evidently he was sane as any man in his therapeutic measures for saving woman from vain regret.

Without transition his fixed enchantment turned to a staggering stare. "*Die Liebe?*—It's the *Strahlen!*" he hooted across to me in the haunted voice of the obsessed.

"Insel," I urged, bewildered, "don't look like that. Your *Strahlen* are evidence of something in you—something noble."

"*So edel—*" I trilled in remembrance of my contact with that flawless spirit. But as if leaping out of himself for once to take stock of an Insel I did not know and as if what he saw was horrible, Insel took that clear, that soaring word and wrapping it in bitterness, hurled it at himself.

"*So edel,*" he echoed, infinitely disabused.

"At all events," I said as a pleasant jolt—"I am going to bring you your suit. You're going to look so fine."

As I passed the table I missed the phosphorescent bone.

"Hadn't you a comb?"

"It's here," said Insel—stretching out a skeletal arm toward the floor—there stood his shoes. In one was stored the white comb. The other was stuffed with a huge white handkerchief. They were his wardrobe.

A warm appreciation stole around my heart for that adorable domesticity of the tramp, which first attracted me, when in my childhood, a clown, taking off his tattered overcoat displayed a wash-hand stand built into the lining.

At that moment my friend Insel was very dear to me.

Then in a sudden I realized how always, and inevitably in attempting to follow it, I must run off the track of Insel's mind—himself unaware that nothing about him could ever stir from a so-mysteriously-appointed place, Insel had retrieved his comb *pour se faire une beauté,* awaiting my arrival with his breakfast!

With a kick of tiny annoyance at a toe of his wardrobe, "Personally, I do not admit the power of the microbe, but if you do—I fear you'll be poisoned," I warned him.

Then I gave him his suit.

When I came in again, Insel was pacing the studio in stealthy meditation. His mischievous assurance was so much his axis and at once so exteriorized that his whole implication seemed to have contracted to the finger of old fashioned comedians pressed to a nose under a crafty eyelid—Insel was feeling so sly— Then, going into reverse—as it was time for him to leave, he began fiddling abstractedly with a gratitude he did not know what to do with. "You have been very good to me," he mumbled shamefacedly. "There is nothing I would not do for you—if *ever*," inspired, "you have a pair of boots which need cleaning."

"Insel," I exclaimed encouragingly, "you needn't say things like that about yourself."

With a jerk he pulled himself out of an underlying complex.

"That was a figure of speech." And inclining towards the couch with the bowing, palm-of-the-hand-drooping invitation with which saints in primitive pictures lead the eye to some sacred center, "Now you be ill, and go to bed so I can nurse you," he pleaded adoringly.

I had to refuse. As I came to think of it, I wouldn't know how to be nursed when ill.

So Insel, as if in prison or barracks, began folding up his sheets and blankets, I took a seat. With the stuff of my cape draping the chair, I felt like an emperor taking pride in a supreme buffoon.

There is no grace on earth to compare with a willowy man afflicted with levitation.

"It's pure selfishness my allowing you to do this. It's up to Bebelle—only I do so enormously enjoy your plastic geometry," I observed to Insel, who, as if fitting a label to perfection, swayed his dreary silhouette of aereal bones, against a lifted sheet bleached in the reflection of his phosphorescence.

"If you want to make a fortune," I advised him, "you should go on the Music Halls— Have you ever heard of Baggesson—one of the geniuses of the century? He broke white plates.

"You are even more wonderful folding white things up—"

"It would be utterly useless," Insel protested. "Nobody ever sees in me what you see in me—"

"Well, you frighten the 'people' out of their wits, that ought to give you a hold on your audience. Of course, you'd need to rehearse— Have someone sit in the back of the theater and tell you *where* you get your effects. You should 'come on' in the fearful chatter of an earthquake and then all you'd have to do would be to leisurely tidy it up— I assure you you'd have the whole theater hallucinated."

When he had stacked up his covers like a deck of cards, there was still one ceremony to perform, I took him into the kitchen and gave him whatever food there was left.

Under my eyes, as he packed it up, it diminished and froze into a Chinese puzzle. The essential, he said, was a minimum bulk. It did not in the least concern me that it would all be thrown away. His tying of the string was the close of a linear symphony.

Insel left with a farewell flash from his cranium

and his forlorn-howl-in-the-wilderness of when shall I see you again— Then he crept back to the door-mat and whispered shyly, "I shall explain everything to you next time."

16

ON MY WAY TO THE STATION I called on Mlle Alpha. In her slacks of rust colored linen—her coppery hair, blown into a fresh sunburn, she appeared to have just sailed in from a lagoon.

Her eyes like coals, continent, of their fire, were round as the eyes of the wooden negresses supporting the violet draperies of her day-bed. Her lacquered toenails played at hide-and-seek among the meshes of her sandals. Her whole body was impudent with a slightly crass adolescence; it centered in her little tummy, which dared to be round.

A hard young apple—it was immediately plain to see, how, had one been on the other side of the fence of sex—one would have wanted to bite into it.

It was Insel who had sponsored our meeting and I gave her his message—that he would keep an appointment at five o'clock.

"He's enthusiastic about you," she said—then, "Would you think me very indiscreet if I asked you what you find to talk to him about for six hours?"

"Oh!" I explained loyally, "we exchange our little anecdotes. There's the girl who went off with the Lesbian—it's stupendous—to halt the endlessness of drama in the mere contemplation of a couple of shots."

"So he tells you that one, too?"

"Look here," I confessed. "At first I was indignant with you for launching the opinion that Insel is mad—. Now I am not sure—. It occurs to me that I can't even make out what sanity is."

"Well, I find him such an awful bore, I am constantly having to turn him out—"

"That's because he's too surrealistic for the surrealists."

But when Mlle Alpha spoke of his work, it was with a profound veneration I could hardly share.

"I'm not so fond of elementals—I find that strata in the subliminal thin—. I know his work is a technical miracle and I submit to the active hypnosis with which he has the power to infuse dead paint—still—. There! That's one thing we're always talking about. His future work. He *shows* me what he is going to do. Sometimes I feel he has found a short cut to consummation in defiance of the concrete. That he is filling the galleries of the increate. He seemed so worth helping, I've only just begun to notice he *never* paints. If he ever does paint the things he sees—God knows *where*—the result will be spectacular."

"Why? Haven't you heard about Insel?" asked

Mlle Alpha. "He and the friend with whom he came to Paris took morphine together and two years ago this friend died. His death gave Insel such a jolt, he dropped the drug, and ever since has painted nothing of any account.

"Why on earth doesn't he take his old morphine?" she demanded of the universe in general, "and let himself die? At least he would have painted his pictures—while this way—where is the good in his remaining alive?"

Now drugs meant nothing to me. I had supposed they were a substitute for imagination in the unimaginative. I was prejudiced against the stories afloat of their awful destructiveness, ascribing them to one of those official dodges for preventing an exasperated humanity from having a little fun. Subconsciously, I waived this information. As if my mind were a jury refusing to be influenced by extraneous evidence. Being thus luckily prevented from putting two and two together, I was free to pursue my investigation of Insel in my own reactive way.

Moreover, was not Insel's morphinism a thing of the past?

17

BEFORE I **LEFT** Mlle Alpha told me that stiff Ussif, the surrealist, had painted a picture I ought to see. Remembering (that under the influence of his feline screech) I had made no appointment with my strange boon companion, I arranged to go to Ussif's the following week on my return to town.

"By the way"—I exclaimed, "I forgot—. When Insel wrote to you—did he predict the day and hour when his resistance must give out—?"

"Nothing of the kind," she answered. "He wrote as usual, 'I am starving to death.'"

When the time came for me to return I arrived to find a telephone message from the dressmaker, who was ill. So I hurried off to do some shopping. Afterwards, on my way to the surealist's studio, I stopped the taxi at my flat to change my gloves.

As I ran up the one flight of stairs, I had to slow down. Surprisingly, on this warm day, an iciness was creeping up my ankles. I proceeded into a chill draught.

"Insel!" I realized.

There was nobody standing at my front door.

Although well lit by a staircase window, it was hung with a square curtain of black mist.

Slowly, this mist put forth an abstract sign of concavity, and still more slowly, a transparent diagram of my friend grew on to it.

Hunching into materialization, as a dead man who should vomit himself back to life, Insel, whose illness was dissolution, moaned to me in the voice of a wraith.

"I thought you would never come."

When I got him inside, we were already laughing—half apologetically—as if we found it absurd, this meeting in no man's land without explanations to offer.

"Why didn't you say you were coming?"

"But I thought—surely—" with an anguished grin, "Friday is my 'little afternoon.' "

"Of course it's your little afternoon, Insel," I laughed. "Only when you have turned the lady down is just when you have to specify the hour of your return; if she is to expect you—I've got an engagement."

"*My* little afternoon," he raved, collapsing, "I was going to take you to my room to see my picture."

18

WHAT *AM I TO DO* with you? The taxi meter is ticking, the surrealist's waiting. Pull yourself together—quick! I'll take you along.

"However did you get that hole in your trousers, it's new—" I demanded, detecting, as we got into the taxi, a perfect round of perforation letting out a tiny light from his thigh. I suspected him of replenishing his beggar's capital.

"It was there before," said Insel sanctimoniously, as if referring to a halo earned by excessive martyrdom.

"You might as well come up and see Ussif with me," I suggested.

"No," said Insel, "none of the surrealists will have anything to do with me. They know only too well, if they did, I should try to borrow money."

"I should have thought you'd be *worth* a little money to a surrealist. He might learn what supereality is about—you are organically surreal—"

"I don't do it on purpose," said Insel dejected.

"I know you don't," I assured him warmly. "You only 'do' Kafka on purpose—you're *so* much better in the original."

I kept my promise of going to his room on my way back. Strangely—the very name of the street he lived in had the sound of a ghostly exhaustion. His attic was on the seventh story.

Along the narrow open passage with its bare iron railing the *Chambres de Bonnes* moved past me as I looked for his name on the doors, when, coming to a closed iron shutter fleeced with dust and cobwebs growing in patches like a moss of soot or hanging in gray festoons about its slits, I felt the liveness of the air decrease, and "Insel" written in the archaic hand of some automatic writings drew up my eyes—. To that darkened crack which outlines the magical versatility of a barrier measuring a yard across and with merely the touch of a hand diminishing to a strip three inches wide. That cover of a living book whose history may come to an end before you can get it open; or cut short your personal adventure by remaining shut; out of this oblong outline of Entrance and Exit there leaked a perceptible seepage of Insel's torpor.

Noiselessly, indolently, the door vanished. I walked into its chasm and Insel led me to his painting set in the pacific light of a large attic window.

"*Das ist die Irma?*" he said with the secretive in-looking twinkle that lit up his eyes with recurrent delights. And suddenly it dawned upon me that one thing about this man that made him so different to other people was that contrary to our outrunning holding-up-the-mirror self-consciousness, his was constantly turning its back on the world and tiptoe with expectancy, peeping inquisitively into its own mischievous eyes. Or, in some cerebral acrobatic recoil, that being who is, in us, both outlooker and window, in him, astonishingly, was craning back to look *in* at the *outlooking* window of himself, as if there were something there he might forget, some treasure as to whose existence he wished to remain assured, some lovely illusion inside him, he *must* re-see to insure its continued projection.

"*Die Irma,*" he repeated lovingly to introduce her to me, and the magnetic bond uniting her painted body to his emaciated stature—as if she were of an ectoplasm proceeding from him—was so apparent one felt as if one were surprising an insane liaison at almost too intimate a moment. He was glittering with a pleasure as dynamically compressed as the carbon of a diamond.

A narrow canvas, nigger-black, whose quality of shining obscurity was the effect of minutely painting in oil on some tempera ground, *die Irma* stood knee-deep on an easel.

To her livid brow, rounded like a half-moon, clung a peculiarly clammy algaeic or fungoid substitute for hair. Beneath it a transparent mask of horizontal shadow was penetrated by the eyes of an hypnosis; flat disks of smoked mirror, having the selfsame semblance of looking into and out of oneself as her creator.

Perhaps in a superfine analysis, this is what all men really do, but as a natural interplay; whereas Insel and his picture were doing it with alternating intent. Indeed the great thin uninscribed coins of her gunmetal pupils, returning his fascinated gaze, were tilted at such an angle as to give a dimly illuminated reflection of an inner and outer darkness.

Her hands, as if nailed to her hips like crossed swords, jutted out from her body which seemed to be composed of rippling lava that here and there hardened to indentations like holly leaves growing from her sternum—her male hands that hardly made a pair, for the one had the bones of the back marked all of equal length and the other, one finger too long with an unmodeled edge which curved like paper against the background.

He hung over *die Irma* like a tall insect and outside the window in the rotten rose of an asphyxiated sunset the skeleton phallus of the Eiffel Tower reared in the distance as slim as himself.

Beside the picture I noticed that the gutter of his upper lip was interrupted by a seam, a fine thread of flesh running from the base of the nose to his mouth that accentuated the compression of his lips in their continual retention of the one remaining tooth which, so thin as to be atavistic in an adult, was like a stump forgotten in a croquet ground, left over from the Game of Life. An incipience or reparation of harelip? And Irma? In this very same spot she puffed to a swollen convergence.

"But Insel," I asked, "her upper lip is about to burst with some inavowable disease. You have formed her of pus. Her body has already melted."

"Exactly," he answered with mysterious satisfaction.

"I don't care for it," I decided.

"And I," said Insel, with the reverent intonement with which he accompanied his tacitly implied admittance of myself to his holy-of-holies, "thought that *this* picture would be just the one that *you* would like."

Time hovered, suspended in the attic air as the powders of life in the noxious mist of the exhausted city below. When suddenly the soporific lure he sowed in his magnetic field—shattered. Insel was snatching at the emptied flesh on his face in the recurrent anxiety inspiring his wilder gestures.

"She ought not to *be*," he cried out, "if you don't like her, I am going to destroy her."

His cerebral excitement seemed to inflate his head, rather as a balloon from which his wasted body hung in slight levitation.

"Come down to the floor, for God's sake," I said peremptorily. "What does my opinion matter? *I'm* not the museum."

"But you're right," he insisted. "I have been going in the wrong direction. *Die Irma's out.*"

"And don't use me as a sop for your terror of working."

"It's really not that—but a technical question. *Die Irma ist nass.*"

"She isn't, she's bone dry. I felt her."

"I assure you, underneath—"

"Every time I've come to Paris you've said the

|| **133**

same thing. Pull yourself together Insel, you've got to finish this for the museum. For you it's work or death. Can't you figure it out?" I urged helpfully— "When you have money and can eat you paint a picture so as to have more money—when you haven't any more money."

"It's more complicated than that," he objected again "*die Irma* is wet—"

I was getting exasperated— When the balls of our eyes caught each other, we both began to laugh.

"If you had heard the Lesbian's synopsis of Frank Harris's confessions, you wouldn't even trouble to mention it—."

"I shouldn't care to read this Lesbian's confessions—it is a Lesbian who has taken the love of my life away from me."

"Well now, I wouldn't mention that either. Of course, it does not matter with me—anybody can tell *me* anything—you know what I mean—when you surrender your arms, chuck them onto neutral territory. I know it's a touch that modernizes your romanticism; all the same, I'd advise you never to make that particular confidence to a woman 'ou connait ça.' "

But Insel was past advice. With a look of dogged emptiness he recited for the *n*th time the story of those *Mädchen* "who shut themselves into the house for a fortnight for fear he would shoot them."

Mostly when speaking of his loves of the past he became quite normal; subnormal really, for his adventures in the actual world had been of an excruciating banality.

As I was also engaged for dinner, I asked the time. Insel who was sitting on a wooden stool stretched out his arm—it reached much further than its actual length would warrant.

Behind the curtain in the corner, carefully secreted under empty boxes, neatly stacked, was his wristwatch. He did not *bring* it out—his arm seemed in some Einsteinian contraction to shorten the necessary distance for focusing the hands.

It was seven o'clock. I took my leave. Insel, astonished as if this were the first break in a timeless conversation, snapped in half; or at least bowed like a poplar in a sudden gale; his dessicated limbs the branches.

Staring vainly towards the door I was opening—he choked in the voice of a Robot, "*Morgen komm ich im Gericht.* Tomorrow I go to court—I am going mad!"

"Then don't forget your little afternoon," I reminded him—"I dote on madmen."

As I was leaving, he seized his palette and dripping an enormous brush into a pile of ebony pigment painted with a heinous neigh of victory, "*Die Irma*——Out!"

19

_MY_ INTERMITTENT INTRUSIONS on Insel's inexplicable Eden of mischief had set their mark upon me. Some of his secretive twinkle had seeped into my eyes and lingered there, eliciting comments from my friends. I became more popular.

Insel, however, did not like it at all—as if I were a thief, a stark sternness shot with flashes of sadism replaced his usual intonations of abased tenderness while, awkwardly enough, I continued to feel myself elfin.

One day when I had returned from a lunch he came in to fetch his "Kafka." I had a good time and prattled to him sociably, "Alceste—the duchess—everyone was intrigued to know why I am so jolly."

"*So lustig,*" Insel hissed—a maniac sadism flaring up in his eyes, and for the first time I saw him as dangerous. "*So lustig,*" his hiss growing shriller and I could feel his hatred twining round my throat as he took a step towards me. But a step no longer the airy step of the hallucinated—it was the pounding tread of the infuriated male. "*Lustig,*" he squeaked, his hiss exhausted.

He approached no nearer. Probably my

absorbed interest in examining his insane pupils dominated him. Anyway, although it now surprises me—it seemed I could not be afraid of him—our "entente" in the visionary lethargy of that primeval chaos we were able to share was fundamental and secure. Confronted with his surface vagaries, I felt at once collected—as if I might have been his "keeper" since the dawn of creation.

"Insel," I said placatingly, "if it would improve your health were I to suffer a hopeless love for you, I'm quite willing. Not today—I have a cocktail party—but some other time, I promise" (thinking of my bouts with the *grand sympathique*), "—you shall see me suffer horridly."

Insel, unconvinced, let out a low growl which sounded like one more *lustig*—while that strange bloom, as if he were growing feathers, spread over his face. He turned into a sugar dove. It flew about the sitting room, dropping from under its wings a three-ring circus. In one ring echoed the cracks of a whip; in one ring rotated an insane steed of mist; and in the other ring Insel's spirit astride an elemental Pegasus—.

"Horror," said Insel and I jumped. "Would I have to grow a *beard* in order to make myself attractive to you?"

The *grand sympathique* (which eventually turned out to be a duodenal ulcer) must inevitably go on the rampage again. Very soon it did. There was no resource to Insel's healing *Strahlen*. Since his screech of a vanquishing cat he had, as far as

I was concerned, subconsciously thrown them into reverse.

For a while I was helpless; then one day when the pain calmed down somewhat, I crawled up to Insel's—still trusting he would finish *die Irma* for America—to give him a hundred francs. That is, I never gave him anything. I am not generous. The few *billets* necessary to keep him going were fully covered by the valuable drawing he had forced me to accept. It would be easy to sell if I needed the money.

It did not occur yet to me how unsuccessfully I had succored him, for when first I met him he had been merely a surrealist—his biography was coherent—steadily since I had "interfered" in his affairs he had grown hallucinatory.

"It's all very well," Frau Feirlein argued with me, "I was here when you advanced him five hundred francs for the Gallery—the very next day he hadn't a sou."

To me it appeared fitting Insel's finances should flicker in and out like himself. For the present no power on earth could dislodge from my mind that luminous effigy of generic hunger—or shake my serene unquestioning insistence on its preservation. Something unknowable had entered into a game with my intuition.

He let me in and returned straight to his needy couch, teetering on the end of his spine in a double triangle as he drew up his knees to replace his feet under cover. I was overcome by a rush of nervous sublimity carried by the air.

"If this is madness," I said to myself, breathing his atmosphere exquisite almost to sanctification, "madness is something very beautiful."

My relinquished conviction of his unutterable value returned as I looked up in the bare swept room. An especial clarity of the light I had noticed before to be associated with his presence was this evening so accentuated I could actually dissect it. Its softly bedazzling quality was not of any extra brightness, but of a penetrant purity that uplifted my eyes. I could discern among the unified flood of customary light an infiltration of rays as a rule imperceptible, filaments infinitessimally finer than the gossamer halo round a lamp in the fog—a white candescence that made the air look shinier, with the same soothing shimmer as candles at mass in sacred houses, only indescribably acute.

I was not unfamiliar with it. That different light I had seen etherealize the heavy features of Signora Machiabene an hour before she was stricken to death. That very essence of light I had begun to perceive during the prolonged moment when a dislocated vertebra had thrown me beyond the circumscription of bodily life.

There is no saying in what bliss consists, yet I could see it incorporated with Insel's face, bathed in that different light, as he lay under his only blanket, his limp hands clasped behind his head.

"I see through the wall," he said, his voice at peace. "I can lie here hour-long watching my neighbors live their dear little lives. Sometimes they play a gramophone and on its way to me the music has become miraculous."

"You have never known ennui," I laughed, forgetting as completely as he evidently had, if indeed he had ever been conscious of, the tortured glowworm of the Boulevard night, the inarticulate confidences of one cut off from mankind; the sleepless seeker after an unmentionable salvation who, blinded by his own unnatural glitter, was so wounded by the dawn; that distracted man who, terrified of isolation, hung onto my hand while he flopped and darted like a fish on the end of a line, stung by a mystifying despair.

"Never," he assented, beatified. "I am eternally content. My happiness is infinite. All the desires of the earth are consummated within myself."

"Aside from that—what are the people in the next room *doing*?"

"Just being—I ask no more of anyone. *Being* in itself is sufficient for us all," he answered enraptured.

Seeing I had taken up one of his drawings, he instantly arose. Always—there was something of the depths of the sea about him and his work, also of eventual evolution as in the drawing I was looking at where to a rock of lava a pale subaqueous weed clung in the process of becoming a small limp hand. The tips of its fingers were stealing into pink.

Insel himself had fearsome hands, narrow, and pallid like his face, with a hard, square ossification towards the base of the back, and then so tapering as if compressed in driving an instrument against some great resistance.

"You were a lithographer, not an engraver?" I had once asked him, puzzled by what his hands looked as if they must have been in the habit of doing, and we concluded this conformation could be an inheritance from the *Schlosser*'s driving power. But out of this atavistic base his fingers grew into the new sensibility of a younger generation, in his case excessive; his fingers clung together like a kind of pulpoid antennae, seemingly inert in their superfine sensibility, being aquiver with such minuscule vibrations they scarcely needed to move—fingers almost alarmingly fresh and pink for extremities of that bloodless carcass, the idle digits of some pampered daughter; and their fresh tips huddled together in collective instinct to more and more microscopically focus his infinitesimal touch. All the same, there was something unpleasantly embryonic about them. I had never seen anything that gave this impression of the cruel difficulty of coming apart since, in my babyhood, I had watched the freak in Barnum's circus unjoin the ominous limpness of the legs of his undeveloped twin.

"Let's have a look at your feet," I said as he came weightlessly towards me. He drew off his slippers, padding over the bare boards on the drained Gothic feet of a dying ivory Christ.

"What's this?" I teased, pointing to a lurid patch on his instep, "a chancre?"

"No, it's only where my shoe rubs me. I bought

new shoes when I sold that picture and they hurt me," he explained, frowning helplessly.

"Why not try pouring water into them and wearing them till they 'adapt'? It often works."

A strange bruise. It shone with the eerie azure of a neon light. But once within range of Insel, nothing seemed unaccountable, as though he submitted to an unknown law enforcing itself through him. Each item of his furnishing, he having touched it, had undergone the precious transformation of the packet he had folded in my home. His hand, in passing over them, must have caused their simple structure to obtrude upon the sight in advance of their banal identity.

A row of powdered-soap cartons, set upon a shelf, he had stood up to the significant erectness of sentinels, their impressive uniforms consisting in the sufficiency of their sheer sides. He showed me they were empty. Altogether his place had an uncommon dignity. Within a stockade of right angles he had domesticated the steady spirit of geometry.

The room, with its two tiny matchboard tables, its curtains of washed-out cotton across an alcove, full of its supplementary radiance, had an air of illogical grandeur beyond commercial price.

20

EVERY NOW AND THEN the sharp of his flickering sadism, a needle occasionally picking up the dropped thread of memory, would prick through his frayed conversation, woven of disjointed themes like an inconsistent lace eked out with stocking darnings.

He recalled my promise—to demonstrate unfortunate love whenever a twinge of pain contracted my features. He peered enthralled at the havoc pain played with me. His delirious peace expanded to full blossom in the smile of Buddha. One felt his utter joy at sight of my disablement had leapt to such a blaze he must melt off it, his fragile person dissolve in his delight, were it not for some mysterious source within him replenishing the exaggeration of his unabating intensity.

"*Gestatten Sie?*" I inquired ceremoniously, unable to hold out any longer against the pathological rat gnawing at my entrails. And I subsided on his couch. Above a certain degree of agony, one is willing to subside anywhere. However, my slight repulsion dispersed as I lay down. Indeed, like the saints whose dead bodies did not decompose, Insel's electric exudation in some process of infinitesimal friction seemed to cleanse him of his grubbiness of the poor, to free him of any accretion natural to normal man. His couch was almost fragrant with that faint half-holy purity that hung about him.

"What color was this once?" I asked, as I drew up his gray blanket.

"White," said Insel.

It was incredible. That twilight sheer duration lowers upon all pale fabrics had so penetrated the thick wool, one could only believe with difficulty it had not been dyed—a perfect job at that—no spot, no smirch, no variation in tone disturbed the unity of its spread surface. For a moment I entertained the idea that Insel had worked all over it with the microscopic point of his lead pencil, for it seemed no earthly dust could defer to such patient order. Anyhow, I decided everything in the place is bewitched, and let it go at that.

Insel, intently keeping watch, had moved his stool some distance away as if to find his range for an inverted "Aim of Withdrawal." Spinning himself into a shimmering cocoon of his magnetic rays, introvert, incomparably aloof, "They're mine," he exulted as clearly as if he were crying aloud.

Too simple to fully imagine the effect of these rays, he had, it would seem, only an instinctive mesmeric use for them. He might even feel them as a sort of bodily loss compensated perhaps by rare encounters with one able to tune in.

"I shall make you some tea," said Insel affectionately, and hushed as a nurse, he began swimming about from his little sink to his wooden shelf—or as a panther softly pacing before a vanquished prey—. I noticed now, as always, whenever one encountered Insel at an angle of meals at home, there was appropriately just enough dust of tea leaves left at the bottom of a packet for brewing the last cup—he would open the door to you holding precisely the fag end of a loaf for the last bite. But today he served a minute carton from an automatic machine in the Metro. Out of it he rolled into my palm a bonbon, virulent green, less than a pea in size.

"Aren't you having any?" I invited, convivial as a gourmet, for in his dimension this was a spread feast and the hot unsavory tea had eased my pain. The very teenyness of his sweetstuff made it more seductive than a giant Christmas cake. But he shook his head impishly in abnegation. I looked inside the carton. There was nothing left.

In the concentrated one-sided luxuriance of our party he evoked his dazzling future—the work he no longer seemed able to do waxed so sublime in his visions (and also in mine as I watched all possible loveliness evolve from his elemental mists, and the creeping to maturity of the almost invisible herbage left from under the withdrawn tide of his hovering waves).

His fame was to be fabulous, his wealth extravagant—so that at last the great Insel would (with a gleam of furtive cruelty for me) marry, as far as I could make out, so increasingly incorporeal he grew in his grand exaltation, my daughter's photograph.

"That will be really nice," I responded genially. "As I come to think of it a son-in-law—."

"Exactly," he burst out wildly. "You and I, we could have such a wonderful time together."

"—a son-in-law with rays—" I brought up short, "—and what would my daughter be doing?" Then hurriedly, thinking to profit him by the occasion, I urged, "You must *paint those pictures*—otherwise, you will grow to be too old to marry her."

"Ah, well," he waived, with that sudden doleful look he had of gazing into an abyss when confronted with whatever imperative of whatever consummation. "No matter! It would suffice me just to know her, to have the joy of *watching* her evolve. It would be a very wonderful thing indeed to take part in the *Entwicklung* of a young creature." And I realized there was nothing, nothing, in all the world elementary enough to serve as object for such simplified observation as his. Everything must henceforth for him drowse in an impotence of arrested development.

This very word, *Entwicklung,* was so much Insel's word; its sound seemed to me onomatopoeic of his intellectual graph. For my alien ear it had a turn of the ridiculous as though a vast process had got twisted in a knot of tiny twigs, haply to unravel and root, and branch against the heavens.

21

I REMEMBERED THOSE STACKS of manuscript he had assured me were at my disposal in the days of "biography." "You promised to show me your notes," I reminded him. "May I not see them now?"

He was coy about his literature, sidling alongside himself in a sort of dual fidget impossible to describe, as if doing sentry duty before his own secrecy.

After a long persuasion he brought out a blotter, the kind for *écoliers* sold in bazaars. Covered in black, stamped with a golden sailing ship, its funereal hue intended for neutralizing ink drops in a kindergarten, this unassuming blotter, the one thing in the place having any tradition, had a decorative air of intruding from a frivolous society. It contained a single sheet of paper which he handed me with great precaution. Very few lines were written upon it. They formed a square block in the center of the page covering little more than the area of a postage stamp.

Hardly had I caught a glimpse, when, "Can you see it?" he inquired suspiciously and snatched it away.

"How could I?" I demurred, "the words are scarcely visible—" Reassured, he gave it back to me.

"You've no idea," he sighed, "the pains I take when I write to you, forcing my hand to form letters big enough for you to read."

"*Liebe* Herr Insel," I cajoled, "*You* read it to *me.*"

At last he did so.

It was a beginning.

" 'My sister and I walked along the road. Coming to the town gate we gave it a good thump.'

"Do you know what a town gate is?" asked Insel professorially. "It's like a tower.

" 'All the townsfolk came out of the gate, swarming about us to look.' "

As ever, with Insel "to look" was a deadlock, he had written no more.

I proffered the necessary compliments. Agog with glee, he shimmered with satisfaction. This communication of an actual transcription of a mental process had reinforced his sociability. His contacts ordinarily depending almost entirely on his *Strahlen,* for the moment our companionship was complete.

In reading aloud his manuscript he had formed an extra alliance with me—as *littérateurs,* producing in Insel an enormous self-respect.

Nevertheless, it was a sympathization going on in some sphere to which I had no access.

Anything he perceived sufficiently to accept or that *thrust* itself upon his attention (as in *my* case) was instantly distilled in his precious essence. Behind his brow a void wraith, glorified, evaporate, dissociated from its originator, myself, to mix with his gaseous cerebration.

Insel let out a shrill crow. *"Es gibt nicht zwei vie Sie—*There are not two like you."

Sparkling, entranced, he sat on his wooden chair as on the throne of the conquistador, for whatever I contributed to his transcendental enjoyment he was loath to let me go.

But I was beginning, myself, to feel unnatural. I distinctly detected my voice in ventriloquial emulation echo the wistful, surf-like swooning singing of his—*"Sterben—Man mu-u-uss—Man mu-u-uss"*—as, worn out with pain, assuring him I must leave because I was tired, I said, *"Ich bin so mü-ü-de."*

Insel, responding to this bemused inflection, or rather, fusing with an ululation so singularly his own it almost obliterated our duality, I witnessed in him an inconceivable reversion of a standard transmutation. The *changing* of *sadism* into *love.* Not gallant love. The indiscriminate love of a savior.

Suffering, I had so gratified him, satiating his sadism—even to extinction, his gratitude refluent to me, enveloped me.

At last with a sacrificial decisiveness Insel consented to let me go. *"Ja,"* he assented, bending over me in solicitude. "Go," he stretched out one of his thin branches in benediction, "Go and sleep." *"Schlafen."* His word was drowsy—so long drawn out. It did not cut the air as ordinary words do. Agelessly sailing, it passed across me—oblong and idle—spacious as an airship, its narcotic cargo a dream of a slumber unknown to normal man.

The rays that Insel so busily had been spinning

around himself in an immeasurable tenderness released, attained once more to me.

Instantly all pain vanished. I sprang up elasticized. To an identical rhythm Insel and I, on a buoyancy, were danced toward the door bobbing and smiling good-bye in a mutual appreciation which I felt must be glittering off me as it did off him.

When I got to the train it was steaming out of the station; casually I skimmed onto it scarcely noticing this, for me, at other times, impossible achievement—I felt so airy. In the car, whenever I thought of Insel, I was shaken with a helpless laughter—a strange mixture of extreme friendliness and, inexplicably, derision.

The painless buoyancy lasted well into the night when, as I sat calmly at work in my hotel bedroom, I unexpectedly disintegrated. My body, which had hitherto made upon itself the impression of a compact mass, springing a multiplicity of rifts, changed to a fractional covering I can only compare to the spines of a porcupine; or rather vibrant streamers on which my density in plastic undulation was being carried away—perhaps into infinity. A greater dynamism than my own rushed in to fill the interstices. Looking down at myself I could *see* my sensation. The life-force blasting me apart instead of holding me together. It set up a harrowing excitement in my brain. An atomic despair—so awful— my confines broke down. I lost contour. Once more I found myself in the "impossible situation" in which one cannot remain—from which there is no issue.

I cognized this situation as Insel's. A maddening with desire for a thing I did not know—a thing that, while being the agent of his—my—dematerialization alone could bring him together again. A desire of which one was "dead" and yet still alive—radial starfish underpattern of his life, it had communicated itself to me. I was being impelled to the pitiable serial choreography of Insel when in the closed cab he had chased himself along the incalculable itinerary of his dissolution.

In a darting anguish consciousness in pulverization peered from the ends of incontrollable antennae for something unattainable.

I had more space than had Insel in his cab, yet the inslanting facade of my room under the eaves with the red glow of its wall paper got "in my way." Having no idea of what was happening to me, I seemed to have also unsuspected reserves of will power. I put up a pretty good fight against this incredible dematerialization—it took me hours to weave myself together—but at last, exhausted yet once more intact, I fell upon my bed and slept.

Next morning my face looked "destroyed" like Insel's.

Although I was all of a piece, my very bones were weak. I had to walk carefully. I found out why, when climbing slowly up the hill to the station to buy a newspaper, I was cleft in half. Like the witch's cat when cut apart running in opposite directions, suddenly my left leg began to dance off on its own. Thoroughly frightened at this bisectional automatism,

I somehow hopped to the fence on my right and clung to it in an absurd discouragement.

The day after that I thought I was normal. Walking serenely at my habitual pace, I went to a shop in the village before keeping an appointment for lunch.

Without association (as usual) the idea of Insel rose in my mind. Quite different to thinking about someone. I was overcome with that imbecilic self-satisfied laughter, that Parnassian guffaw. It had nothing to do with any humor known to the intellect; being a sort of blank camouflage for all intellection. With me it was always filtered with a faint derision. But even this derision I took for granted. Brought to a halt under the full force of my mental hilarity, I felt constrained to *continue to share it*—with what?—with whom? To do so I turned sideways. Whenever this *idea* of Insel occurred I could not go straight ahead—I had to turn to it—as when I had tried to sum him up on the Boulevard.

My feet remembered that lightness, that skimming of the pavement—I was engrossed in a merriment beyond existence. When this merriment ceased, I found myself in a part of the country I had never seen before.

I had kept track of the time to avoid being late—as that gust of laughter caught me it had been twenty to one. I walked into an open yard where a man was washing a car. He informed me it was twenty to one and that it would take me half an hour to get back to the place where by all the laws of possibility

I should still have been. He allowed me to telephone my friends, to begin lunch without me, that I had got lost—at the other end of the wire it was twenty to one.

All this was comparable to an incident that occurred when I made friends with a little girl whose intelligence was like a jewel in a case too tightly closed. A backward child, one of those partial imbeciles, who, not being "all there," showing only half their human nature, are either angelic or diabolic. Probably their own halves are all they respond to in other people, for Fifi, when she said "*Bonjour*" with a smile of benediction, would discover, "Madame, you are as sweet as a rose."—"Monsieur, you are bright as gold." Her being subnormal lent an elfin prestige to her slow serenity among her associates, offspring of peasants and small tradesmen, who attended the informal court she held in the parlor behind her parents' shop.

Rigid as bygone queens in her orthopedic corset, she accepted the offering of every conceivable kind of toy duck from her wondering courtiers, with a lunar giggle that never precisely applied to anything. Her passion, her concretion of sublimity, took the form of a duck. "God is playing hide-and-seek," she would announce, "so the Virgin Mary has married a duck and they live in the top story of the Riviera." And once when I found her watching some live water fowl by a pond in a farmyard—"Why do you love the duck?" I asked her. "*Il dort dans son dos*," she perfectly replied.

A fearful future opened before her if she could never keep shop, and the medical specialists consulted on her behalf promised she would become like average children should they graft a bit of the bone in her leg as a wedge into her spine, thus rectifying her crookedness and relieving the pain. But this operation, successful they said in many other cases, failed with this half-wit angel, who, incidentally, had predicted the year of her own death.

So Fifi died most uncomfortably, lying very much like a trussed duck, only on her tummy—her leg being bent up behind her for the grafting and bound to her back—screaming in a nursing home until she had no more breath.

Only once, in talking to this little girl, had I seen her unhappy. An unhappiness intense as it was brief. A drip of anguished words revealing how she received as an awful animosity her mother's solicitous efforts to get her to "make sense."

While undressing to go to bed that night, as if a flash of sympathetic insight "put me in her place," I suddenly found myself imprisoned in Fifi's mind.

Strangely enough, it was analagous to my sensation of utter helplessness when dislocating my cervical vertebra, I had found myself without any instrument with which to contact the universe.

But now I was at the mercy of an imperfect instrument. The antennae of the contact with the world in some way crippled for their function seemed—like the umbilical cord in abnormal birth—to be wound round my brain in a fearful constriction, implacable as iron barriers.

My brain, like a bird in ceaseless hurt, beat its wings for the conscious liberation against a cage—or rather, a sort of immature sieve, which would spring a hole intermittently; here and there letting a glimpse of phenomena through—phenomena fitful and unrelated.

Caught in a horror of active impotence, I struggled in terror—unlike Fifi, I could get out.

This gratuitous experience was as nothing to that of disintegration when, on the contrary, one became aware of *forces* inherent to phenomena, which, being beyond the range of registration by the normal instrument—the conscious organism as it exists in our present stage of evolution—resulted in a super-sensibility so acute it shattered itself to splinters.

The intuitional self is incapable of surprise, but my everyday self was amazed. I felt that for dabbling in the profane mysteries I had got more than was coming to me.

Less than anything on earth did I require a face destroyed as Insel's; for some while I should walk with misgivings—.

I racked my brain for an explanation of my soaring respect (respect being a sentiment foreign to me) for a loafer who in the light of common sense proved to be actually silly.

Insel, who, so sensible of his essential mystery— communicated that sense of imminent magic inevitably, just when one was in the "thick" of his influence would illustrate his "power" with a story such as how, after dining with married friends, he had predicted to his wife, "*That* union will not last long."

"*Und Tatsächlich,*" he concluded with an expression of awe, "they separated within the year."

He suffered, it would seem, from the incredible handicap of only being able to *mature* in the imagination of another. His empty obsession somehow taking form in obsessing the furnished mind of a spectator.

From a distance one remembered him vaguely as an indulgence in a quaint innocuous vice. Still I could scarcely go further with him than dissolution. I decided it would be useless to see him again.

My brain still seemed to be vibrating out of time, when early one evening on leaving a library I wandered into an old church. Somebody up in the organ loft was playing Bach. A sublime repetitive patter of angels' feet soled with assuagement, giving chase to one another in a variable immobility of eternal arrival, they trod my cerebral vibrations from disarray into tempo once more.

I had not thought of my casual prediction that the whole of Insel's life would hang upon a key— when on mislaying my own key to my apartment he produced the duplicate I had lent him in the days of his "eviction"—and *forgot* (the place was still at his disposal) to ask me for it again.

It was a long while before it occurred to me that his girl's watch was lying at the jeweler's. By then, all that remained of Insel was a vague impression of *trompe l'oeil*. I wrote him to call for this love relic, he having assured me that should I have it sent to his address his concierge would seize it towards arrears in rent.

Insel, an eroded scarecrow, greeted me with the somber dignity of a dejected god.

"Why did your girl give you such a rotten watch," I teased, "the jeweler won't guarantee it."

"One takes what one can get," said Insel with no trace of emotion as I had handed him the erstwhile "Adam and Eve in primeval embrace." His present concern was for getting back the key. Determined he should not have it, I pretended I was returning to Paris.

Lolling on either end of the great couch, supported by our elbows, our feet on the floor, we were at ease for conversation—the conversation would not begin—Insel being taken up with contracting to some intense concentration that gradually pushed out a sort of pallid ethereal moss to cover his ravaged face.

At last, to my raised eyebrows, "*Ah, liebe* Frau Jones," he complained in prayerful peevishness, "it's not so easy for me—I don't mean anything to you anymore."

"I know," I said contritely, "I get these wild enthusiasms for things—they don't last."

"And we might have had such a wonderful time together," he sighed.

22

I COULD NOT MAKE out why this fantastically beautiful creature should have both hands round my throat, when Insel, shrunken to a nerve, his eyes fixed as blinded granite, sat at that distance with his fists so tightly clenched. Fingers of automatic pressure rapped their tonnage of abstract force on my jugular—the blood on my brain surged in a noisy confusion—"You are going to give in—obsessed by my beauty—having no hope—endlessly resigned—"

All the air wheezed in my exploding ears as a last breath, "—suffering—suffering—suffering—choked by a robot!" This was not all that suffocated me—myriads upon myriads of distraught women were being strangled in my esophagus.

I had known exhaustive desperation but no such desperation as this—with its power of a universal conception—of limitless application: being impersonal made it the more overwhelming.

"You—are—going—to—give—in."

"To whom?" I wondered—my eyes closing. "To Insel? Or this incredibly lovely monster made of dead flesh."

"Thou art fair my beloved, thou—," rose from a subconscious abyss.

Not wholly convinced I wrenched my eyelids apart—my cerebral current, flowing an infinitessimal fraction of a second faster than the normal, registered Insel. I caught him at it. Swift as the leaves of the shutter on a camera when a snapshot is taken, there came together upon his concentric face a distinct enlargement of Colossus' photograph that always stood on the sitting room mantlepiece at the other end of the flat.

Simultaneously it came back to me how Insel, on his first visit, had taken that photo between his hands to stare at it inordinately as if for reproduction, for a long time, and at length bringing it nearer to his eyes.

"Such beauty as this," he said, "could scarcely happen more than once in a hundred years." He himself put it at two thousand, I had laughingly observed.

"Stop it," I commanded, letting fly a fearful kick at Insel's brittle shin. As if he were anaesthetized, the kick seemed not to hurt him—he received it with the smile of ultra-intimacy he had for me whenever we met on the unexplored frontiers of consciousness.

"The pet! The lamb!—it does television, too," I told myself delightedly.

"Insel," I laughed, enthusiastic over him once more.

"*Seien wir uns wieder gut*—I give you the key— dinner—My man Godfrey—the loan on your picture

—you go to the Balkans—you are the living confirmation of my favorite theories."

As for Insel, he emerged from his "raptness" babbling of Colossus—Colossus as he had himself foretold me having taken on an immortality as an evergrowing myth. Insel claimed him as a kindred spirit with ideas identical with his own.

"How entirely he would have accepted me—my art— We would have been as one—"

I argued at length against this sudden conviction. "Do you know," I asked, "who, for the so-called precursor of surrealism, was the supreme painter?—Rubens—" Only then did Insel's illusions miserably dissolve.

23

AFTER THE POWELL FILM, we instinctively returned to Montparnasse—eating at a chic bar. The barman and Insel behaved as brothers—I vaguely noted a sort of ritual—the passing and repassing between them of half a cigarette. They addressed each other as "du." "No—for 'thee'—" Insel would say, placing the stump on a glass shelf as one handles a treasure.

Some days later I saw this barman out of doors

wearing one of the richest overcoats I had seen in Paris. Evidently such acquaintances could hand out "leavings" superior to the plain nourishment Insel acquired from the Quakers.

We sat around the Dôme and Insel x-rayed. All the girls, as they giggled along the Boulevard, he disrobed—more precisely, he could not *see* that they were dressed. As if on an expedition for collecting ivory, he *handed* me their variously molded thighs—weighed them with an indescribable sensitivity of touch.

"This one," he assured me, "in the summer is firmer—turns to gold—"

Recalling how terribly Mlle Alpha had said he dated, I presumed he was claiming my interest by indulging in what Boulevardiers of the old days called "undressing the women" in his own unbelievably tangible way. "I don't *need* them to take off their clothes," he remarked.

In the Select Insel became actually involved with his watching of a red-haired girl he raved of as "*die Rothaarige*"—her thighs were peculiarly long and agile. "She's a bit of a Lesbian," he sighed, filled with some inverted reminiscence of antagonism.

"Look here, Insel—you're crazy about that girl—and all you do is sit around x-raying her—Get up—go and speak to her—"

"She'd be too expensive—"

"Colossus never had any money."

"Colossus was beautiful—"

"What about it? You're looking unearthly. She might get a thrill out of it—try—forget the expense—I'll back you— Go along."

But Insel, subsiding in his inexplicable negativism, refused to stir.

"Listen," I admonished him, "all this is really unwholesome—and sitting boxed up in an attic adoring that canvas Irma all day—you'll become impotent—"

In a burst of the extravagantly sophisticated laughter I had heard him emit once before, "I only wish I could," he assured me.

"What a subject," I reflected, "the virility of the starving man." But the Select was undergoing change—opening out to aqueous space in darkling shadows of metallic liquidity as in the vision of the Lutetia, that strangely etiolate phallic ghost floated like the stem of a water lily. Before it had terminated in a battlement akin to that of the castle among chessmen; now it was topped with a little crown of thorns.

Through the chill shimmer of this unreal deep—the hallucinatory blue the Coupole had painted on the backs of dreary houses as a setting for its garden cafe—the blue I would wish the sky to be showed us another dawn.

"Look."

"There should," said Insel, extremely worried, "be a lighted lamppost there."

"There is," I reassured him, "lower your head—see it was cut off by the blind."

This was the last of the two or three nights I spent with Insel in Montparnasse.

We crossed again to the Dôme to have breakfast. Sitting beside him, I could see a man in white armor conduct a ballet. Serried rows of mustard pots drew up before him, their porcelain bellies burdened with amber. They moved to and fro as with a wooden spatula he lifted off their stale crust of night, filled and leveled them, and set each one down to be armed with a clean bone spoon.

"*Woher kommt diese halbe Mücke?*" Insel grumbled, insanely hacking with his knife at a tiny aeronaut shade circling an inviolate orbit, because he could not make out "Where this half a fly comes from." I knew it was only a baby fly, yet all the same it loomed above him hugely as an insectile cherubim cut off from its entrails in a like unanatomical constipation to Insel's monsters.

The rest of the day till two o'clock when Insel, as usual, it seemed must "appear in court," we spent in an incredibly concentrated and somehow heart-rending arithmetic, reckoning up whether Insel, out of the three thousand francs loaned on his picture, could possibly afford a new pair of boots. We had already decided he must have a warm overcoat when, although it was not particularly chilly, little muscles in the side of Insel's nose, self-animated, leapt up and shivered. "You are freezing," I discovered in startled concern, scanning his fragile flimsy features.

"I hardly feel it—I am used to it," said Insel,

dolefully heroic. "It is only discomforting to those who are with me."

But I teased him a bit when we said good-bye, alluding to a lunch with the Alpha when to our mutual hilarity we had made out how only two hours after leaving my studio after that utter collapse, he had stumbled into hers.

"He looked *ghastly,*" she told me. "He had not eaten, he had not slept—his heart had ceased to beat!"

Insel, whom I had seen so sly, had been vainly hoping to get his beefsteak fresher.

"How on earth," I inquired, "do you compose your *Totenkopf* in so short a time? Pretending to Mlle Alpha—"

"Why," Insel answered pat, with the queerest inflection of intimacy, as if I were some virgin he had raped, "I thought you would not *like* me to tell her I had *been with* you."

"It's marvellous," I assured him in amused admiration, "your knack of dying on doorsteps. At will! At any moment! You might make a good thing out of it. Perhaps you do. Insel, I believe you put *lots* of money in the bank!"

I could feel a distinct change in his aural temperature, but I was laughing too much to pay attention. An impression of a sacred stronghold "blowing up," that shadow-tower of iron rag the *clochard*-deity Insel had built, like an ant of his wasted tissue, was so very, very faint—

In view of America, I was constantly on the

hop—busy with buyers of furniture—packers littering the place with straw.

Arriving for some appointment, I was unprepared to run into an Uneasiness in the vicinity of my home, although it remained closely sealed in its shutters and nothing by day ever went in or came out. *Les concierges,* their aides and cronies, the grocers at the corner, all were under the apprehension of the place being haunted. Even Bebelle, whom I came across in the street, had, on going there to clean, turned and fled.

"Madame," she said in a hushed warning, "in there it is dark at noon. Terrible clothes have clotted on the floor— Never before have I seen what was lying on the bed."

Insel at last must have been evicted and at some unknown hour crept into the flat.

24

SOMEONE WAS LIVING THERE.

On my throwing open a window, he hooked his arm round his neck, rubbing the mastoid. "I have lain here for two whole days," he said, ferocious with dignity. "I have a stiff neck."

A hard-eyed, low class German, his very

existence an insolence, wearing a shirt from a cheap shop—Insel must have thrown himself away with his old black sweater above which his former face had risen like a worn, pocked moon.

Unquestionably, I had cured him. Here was the "normal" man. An Insel unobsessed. Someone "replacing himself," his mesmeric, melodic voice exchanged for a hostile creak.

This culminating phase of my eerie experience —Insel's *residence*—remains confused, as I was busy directing packers.

Cavilling and bilious, whenever he caught sight of me he hardly refrained from spitting. Our relative positions entirely reversed, I had become for him a strange specimen, to whose slightest gesture he pinned an attention like that of a vindictive psychiatrist.

"Ha-ha!" he neighed irately, "I find little 'still life' in this flat. It would surely be of the greatest interest to Freud."

We had, in our "timeless conversation," with Insel's concurrence in my "wonderful ideas," superseded Freud. I must always have known he had never the slightest idea of what I was talking about—yet only now did this fact appear as negatory.

The still life that intrigued him was a pattern of a "detail" to be strewn about the surface of clear lamp shades. Through equidistant holes punched in a crystalline square, I had carefully urged in extension, a still celluloid coil of the color that

Schiaparelli has since called *shocking* pink. Made to be worn round pigeon's ankles for identification, I had picked it up in the Bon Marché.

Out of this harmless even pretty object an ignorant bully had constructed for me, according to his own conceptions, a libido threaded with some viciousness impossible to construe.

I was astounded.

It would be only natural that my jerky vibrational currents (which behave so much like a "poltergeist" that things when I touch them are apt to vanish, adding a superhuman difficulty to my work) should impinge on Insel's abnormal precision with the force of a shock, although in the hallucinatory dimension it was this very extreme of antithesis that must set up the telepathic, televisionary machinery of our reciprocity.

"What do you suppose," hissed my horrid guest, who somehow behaved like an alienated husband, "would happen to me if I were to lose anything?"

"Oh, I suppose," I countered rudely, "I'd buy you another."

Being the intrinsic complement of Insel's enmity, logically my loathing for the real man was unconcealed, while he must actually hold himself in check not to assassinate me, for no crueller abhorrence could ever issue from the human heart than Insel's for me.

There were brief abatements of his fantastic normality as when on coming up from the telephone

I encountered only a creature of pathos in the hall.

"You would not notice, would you," wistfully, "that I have polished everything in the flat."

"No," I concurred, "I would not have noticed that."

Insel was long in swallowing his disappointment, then cryptically, "*Gut,*" he snapped, "and I am always amorous when drunk."

And again, for fear I might forget the loan, Insel went limp as he had to the air raid siren. That unaccountable bloom he put forth when passing from one condition to another made his features appear to be of crumpled velvet.

Sitting on a chair of average height, he seemed to have sunk to bottomless depths, at the same time his imploring face peered at me—from the floor.

Craven to a degree that rendered his cowering august, of that meekness befitting a supplicant at the door of heaven, Insel was knowing an alibi so sublime—I again lost all knowledge of who he was.

"Here," I hailed the will-o'-the-wisp, "after all I will give you the little box." This box he desired, it was black, was a small object by the American surrealist, Joseph Cornell, the delicious head of a girl in slumber afloat with a night light flame on the surface of water in a tumbler, of bits cut from early *Ladies' Journals* (technically in pupilage to Max Ernst) in loveliness, unique, in Surrealism— the tidal lines of engraving cooled its static peace. Under the glass lid a slim silver slipper and a silver ball and one of witch's blue came raining down on the gray somnolence when one lifted it up.

I should have preferred to keep it myself had I not suddenly realized she belonged in those idle hands to which the unreal Insel intermittently returned.

I only went twice to the flat while Insel was living there, but I flitted in and out so busily—those hours retain no sequence. As part of his loan I had arranged for a strictly non-negotiable ticket and brought him a first thousand to speed the acquisition of that overcoat.

Insel was completely cured of his obsession. I have never known any man to catch so many women. He seemed to be somehow barricaded with women. All my indulgence for human misdemeanors (which are so commendable when aesthetically good—such as the stellar combine of Insel and his ebony wives, his ivory eroticism in appraising thighs) was unavailing, confronted with this blatant lubricity of the normal Insel which, as he boasted, although in proper decency of word, seemed as did once an astral Venus to flow in his very veins: The dregs of all the secret gutters that carry off the unavowable residue of popular conceptions of physical life—

When I arrived with the rest of the loan, anxious to clear him out, my once luminous *clochard* had composed himself in the kitchen holding his usual insignia, the heel of pumpernickel, this time one in either hand—extreme oval ends—unbitten—of an absent loaf. He looked forbidding as had they been bone.

"Did you get the overcoat," I inquired amiably.

"I may as well tell you," he snarled, "that I don't care for all this supervision—I had not the time. You understand—the last nights in Paris," he raved ecstatically. "*Es ist so schön das Leben, wenn mann so leben kann*— It is so beautiful living, when one can so live."

His emaciation no longer of flesh had become an exteriorized act of the flesh in which the last ooze of the spermatic juices might have been, in some fearful enervation, spent. Instead of being suffused with that liquidity of relief following upon embrace, his eyes, in some ultimate heat, were boiled to the creamy, soiled putrescence of stale oysters in a stew.

I did not reflect that this enormity of sensuous filth was probably as unreal as his nervous aromatics distilled from his astral collusions with a goddess. It was a mental impossibility to associate these opposite phenomena. Had I recalled the earlier iridescent Insel, it could only have been as a figment of *my* insanity.

An alarming presentiment occurred to me. "Insel," I gasped, "you've blown that thousand francs."

"What are you?" he sneered venomously, "an inquisitor?"

"He has notions as to how white women should be handled, too," I laughed to myself as I hurried down the corridor to the dressmaker.

I was determined to take conventional leave of a guest who would be gone when I returned to Paris. It would put me to great pains, I supposed, breaking through animosity so unaccountable it left nothing intact but surprise. Still, it was pretty bad if I could not prevent the "epidemic quarrel with me" from spreading to even this lunatic whose essential void I had found so soothing.

After my fitting I invited him to come down to the cafe, intent on buttering him up, on bluffing him into forgetfulness of having allowed me to discover his awful alter ego (in cases of the sane, this alter ego seldom got to work until out of my sight), curious to see if we could part on good terms.

As we stood face to face with nothing in common, the last people on earth likely to become acquainted, I saw him force back his loathing, to accept. Our mutual distaste was noxious on the palate. We each had a pressing engagement for dinner.

I remembered Geronimo taunting me that I was "no psychologist." "You just walk into a man's brain, seat yourself comfortably in an armchair to take a look around—afterwards, you write down all you have found there," he had said. Then what the hell in Insel had I "walked into"? His complaint was true. Nobody saw in him what I saw in him. A kind of consciousness unconscious of its own potency. Even now he was disgusting to the point of revelation.

Insel had also the idea of bluffing a conformative wind-up to our illusory alliance. Resorting to his earlier priggish decency, once we were in the back of the cafe, he hung his head, apparently poisoning it with spurious shame, and mumbled: —

"The bad thing about me is that every now and then I come to a blind alley in my life—where somebody has to help me."

"Now look here, Insel," I persuaded him with stimulant hypocrisy, "if it were not for that basic something in you—no help would be forthcoming. That which is valuable one does not *help,* one responds to a cosmic imperative."

He began to look as if he had been overdoing the shame.

"There was some mention," I added offhandedly authoritative, "of you busting a thousand francs. You seemed on the defensive. But *why?* The artist requires *color* in his life." This fallacious insight melted Insel's imitation shame, disclosing the very really wounded face of a child who has long been sulking for being misjudged.

"You told me," he burst out unhappily, writhing with reproach, "that I put lots of money in the bank."

So that was it. Insel, with his organic magnifications, had become a foul lout, because he was feeling—cross.

"I didn't," I fibbed, striking the suitable note. "I said you hid it under the carpet." Neither of us had a carpet—we immediately floated off as if on the magical mat of Baghdad, talking on—.

I could feel any word I was saying fit into Insel's brain appeasing as a missing piece in a jigsaw puzzle.

At once—it was growing late—he clamored for me to stay with him; for that period in which alone he seemed to recognize duration—forever.

Probably I was the collaborative audience to his finest act, the giving off of that calm equation that always reduced me to a hushed respect. He grew in power in his silent "role" in ratio to my reaction. The ultimate self, august in certainty, put forth a soporific bloom that covered his damaged face.

Only now I remarked that on the emergence of this ultimate self in its intangible armor of nobility depended that prolongation of time I so often experienced in the company of Insel, for at present there was no aquarium diffusion, none of that virtually giggling attainment to Nirvana. No x-ray excursion nor any fractionation. His mediumship concentrated in a sole manifestation. This interference with time.

I could not make out whether the cause was a shift in the relative tempos of a cosmic and microcosmic "pulsation," whether *my* instant—the instant of a reductive perceiver—passed through some preponderant magnifier and enlarged, or whether a concept (become gnarled in one's brain through restriction to the brain's capacity) unwinding at leisure, was drawing my perception—infinitely soothed—along with it. For again this novel aspect of time seemed, like light, to arrive in rays focusing on the brain at a minimum akin to images on retinas; and the further one projected one's being to meet it, the *broader* one found it to be. Anyway, it was useless trying to analyze it. This alone was certain. It was absolutely engrossing to the mind, although nothing brief enough for us to cognize *happened* in this longer time, which occurred commensurately with the bit of lingering I was wedging in for Insel between contiguous hours in defiance of occupational time.

Rarely, at intervals of aeons, Insel and I would look up at each other in an utter yet somehow communicative impersonality, the final relationship of distinct similars confronting the same phenomenon.

25

INTIMATELY CONFIDENTIAL once
more, Insel was trying to disentangle before me *the thousand directions.* He had shown them to me previously, in answer to my asking him why he did not work although I had left him materials in my studio.

"So often at dusk I come here to stare at that white canvas," he had told me dreamingly. "I see all the worlds I could paint upon it. But *um Himmels Willen!* Which one? I can create everything. Then what thing? A thousand directions are open to me, to take whichever I decide—I cannot decide."

I had long ago worn down in contemplation of that multiplicity of direction. How *far* my mind had traveled; never to come to the *beginning* of any route. Surely, for Insel it should have been different—starting with the spectral spermatozoa that seeped from his brain through his gardening hands.

The glare in Capoulards Cafe grew dim. Insel's brain floated up from his head, unraveled, projected its convolutions. They straightened in endless lines across a limitless canvas, a map of imminent direction. On the whole of space were only a few signboards on which grew hands, alive and beckoning.

"Of course," I was saying, "I don't know where you are—wherever it is is very far away. And I am just as far away. I have existed before my time."

"How true," said Insel.

"Whatever I have found out belongs to a future generation."

"How true," said Insel again, devoutly.

"And by the bye," I commented, "the sentiment of one generation is the neurosis of the next. All that stuff you have of 'suffering for love' is the most awful slush."

"I know—I know," he agreed with fervor.

—Indefinable lines of cerebral nerve marked on the map of inertia, unrealizable journeys. Along one route, *die Irma* dissolved to a puddle of serum, to be absorbed by the all-pervasive whiteness. To travel there was difficult; that volatile fungoid lichen outcrept one as one picked one's way, grew tall until one must turn back.

My former trust in the ripening of Insel's work had had its foundation in that very "parting of the ways" he told me he had come to, where he turned assured toward something eternally immune to his host of elementals.

It had taken so short a time for this parting of the ways to subdivide into the thousand directions. Yet even now he was rich in postponement. While that commonplace back of a woman watching for signs on his painted firmament turned in anonymous patience to this chart of unarrival.

The curtain of the sky came down and she was not there—"If the painting no longer 'goes,' " Insel surprisingly was ruminating, "I shall do as you do. Write. What a profession. One carries one's studio about with one. A sheet of paper—"

Because it was only a brain that had been spilled, the blank of orientation faded—the thousand directions withdrew, leaving us at a destination.

Nothingness.

It was not black as night nor white as day, nor gray as death—only a nonexistent irritation as to what *purposed inconsequence* had led us into the illusion of ever having come into being.

The haunting thing about this Nothingness was that it knew we were *still there*— Two unmatched arrows sprung from its meaningless center—were surrounded by a numeral halo—I *had* to leave Insel, it was ten to eight.

26

HOW GOES THE BOOK," he asked with his

former appreciative intimacy as we passed out of the cafe. I was feeling exceptionally "good" about my work just then, vainly imagining I had criticized my last incompletion.

"It is going wonderfully," and with a flash of that exhibitionism of the spirit succeeding to inordinate periods spent with no means of communication—I threw out my hands—elatedly believing I had reached the stage prescribed by Colossus for creation, when all that one has collected rolls out with the facility of the song of a bird.

"*Sehen Sie*, Insel," I explained, "*Man muss reif sein*—One must be ripe."

I felt Insel crack as if he had been *shot* alert.

"Can she possibly mean it," I could "*hear*" him ask himself as he wheeled towards me, noticing *me* for the *first* time; and then convinced, as I stood a little exalted on the corner of the street, decide, "Here is a woman with whom there is absolutely *nothing* to be done."

I must have had my hands outspread, for Insel dropped like a soft moth into my open palm— On his face was a smile unlike all the fluctuant smiles of hallucinated angels I had watched there. It was a normal smile. Yet in the old abnormal voice of whispering emotion, laying his dried branch across my shoulder, he choked, *"Ich komme nach Hause."*

He was "coming home."

Across his gentle brow floated the will-o'-the-wisp trailing a pair of boiled oysters in its wake, *Mädchen*, like missiles that have not gone off, he scattered abroad.

"But Insel," I reminded him, "you have an appointment for dinner."

Insel gaped at me.

The illocal foci of his pupils exploding incredulously, darted in all the directions of the radial underpattern of his life. It took some moments to sort these simultaneous impressions. When I had done so, I longed to get even with Insel, to say "I have absorbed all your *Strahlen. Now* what are you going to do?"

I said nothing of the kind. Because firstly it was not true, and secondly, it might inspire in him a worse obsession; for one thing one feared as above all else menacing Insel was some climax in which his depredatory radioactivity must inevitably give out.

So all I said was "Good-bye."

"Good-bye," smiled Insel, his bittersweet stare both dazed and stoic, *"Danke für alles*—Thanks for everything."

Afterword

INSEL IS A NOVEL written by a poet, with a poet's interest in the sounds of words. What is at first most striking, and of special interest to readers of Loy's poetry, is the adamantine, alliterative quality of the language here which, like the slow piling up of latinate diction and byzantine phrasing in her poems, makes Loy's novel difficult. But what may on first reading seem byzantine and unapproachable is the very quality which gives Loy's writing an austere beauty that repays the attentive reader. Choosing the most resistant subject matter, and employing language at once stony and visionary, she finds beatitude in the most unlikely places. Insel the *clochard*, the ethereal bum, belongs to a long line of materially destitute characters in whom Loy located spiritual riches.

The arduous language with which she develops Insel's character reflects a decision to persist in the struggle to hammer the ineffable out of the hard physical matter of language, paint, stone and metal that were Loy's media as a poet and visual artist. The narrator's fear for Insel, and for herself as she comes under his spell, derives from Insel's disengagement from the physical world, which—in spite of its imperfection—provides the material for art. Although she is repeatedly tempted to join Insel on his flights into the "increate," lured by her glimpses of beauty in the perfect peace of his vision of the absolute, she is ultimately repelled by the way this vision turns one away from life rather than toward it. Her resolve to fight Insel is remarkable given the force with which his vision attracts her: "If Insel committed suicide—I could share in that, too." The promise of a blissful reprieve from life's suffering proves almost too great a temptation for the narrator, who later will need to weave her disintegrated self back together after an outing with Insel.

But just as the mantras of "timeless peace," "perfect happiness," blooming fragrance and space are about to pull her under, she happens to glance at a cafe clock, on whose "uncompromising dial all things converged to normal." "In my veritable seances with Insel, the clock alone retrieved me from nonentity—thrusting its real face into mine as reminder of the temporal." This periodic attention to the clock prevents her from merging with the otherworldly Insel, who seems to be on his way out of life, having relinquished his right to secular existence. Frequent appointments with friends and other artists—a relentless schedule—provide a structure within which the narrator can both experience Insel's world from a safe distance and maintain the balance necessary to record her experience of his

"Edenic region of unreasoning bliss," which in spite of its destructiveness she values. In her description, Insel visualizes "the mists of chaos *curdling into shape*," just as she herself seeks to evoke "a chaos from which I could draw forth incipient form." The narrator consistently pushes the "procreational chaotic vapor" that threatens to destroy both Insel and herself in the direction of artistic form. It is no surprise, then, that the narrator's final victory over Insel—the definitive moment of the book—coincides with her success as a writer. By the end of the novel, she has reached the necessary compromise for the practicing artist: to make the most of the flawed human condition, to refine as much as possible the imperfect media available to the artist in this world. She encourages Insel to do the same, to get back to his painting in spite of both his financial worries and his precarious hold on reality. But she can only be sure that she herself will keep her balance; she leaves Insel at last to fend for himself.

Insel, the character, is modeled on the German surrealist painter, Richard Oelze, with whom Loy was acquainted in the mid-1930s in Paris. Rumor has it that Oelze was addicted to opium, and that Loy may have helped him recover from his addiction. Though in *Insel* and many of her poems Loy focuses on how decadence incapacitates the artist, she also makes a point to cast in sharp relief the actual devastation of individual lives brought about by drug addiction, poverty, and madness. Throughout her writing career, Loy gravitated toward the

rockbottom of human existence for her subject matter, always struggling to locate what beauty or hope
might reside there, but without romanticizing the
anarchy or squalor.

Mina Loy met Oelze in 1933. By this time, she had
already written two other fictional accounts of
avant-garde figures she knew, neither of which was
ever published. *Brontolivido* satirizes the Italian
Futurist, F. T. Marinetti, and *Colossus* describes her
relationship with Arthur Cravan ("Colossus" in *Insel*),
the proto-Dadaist poet whom she married in 1918.
During the twenties, Loy had associated with several
other expatriates living in Paris, including Ezra
Pound, James Joyce, Natalie Barney, Djuna Barnes,
Gertrude Stein, Constantin Brancusi, and Peggy
Guggenheim (probably "Alpha" in *Insel*), who
helped Loy financially, arranging exhibitions of her
art work and backing her lamp shade business for
a time.

From 1931 until she left Paris in 1936, Loy worked
as Paris representative for her son-in-law, Julien
Levy ("Aaron" in *Insel*), an art dealer and collec-
tor whose New York gallery introduced surrealist art
to America. Her job was to commission paintings for
the gallery from artists, such as Oelze, who were living in Paris. Earlier associations with Marcel
Duchamp, Cravan, and Man Ray had given her
entrée to André Breton's circle of surrealist artists in
the twenties, and she successfully commissioned
work for Levy's gallery from Max Ernst, Salvador
Dali, René Magritte, Alberto Giacometti, Giorgio de

Chirico, and other major figures of the movement. Chances are that it was in this capacity that Loy met Oelze, who arrived in Paris on the last train out of Hitler's Germany and, 33 years old and relatively unknown as a painter, continued an itinerant lifestyle that ended only after the war, when he settled in Worpswede. Around the time Loy knew him, he seemed always to be passing through the places he lived in, invariably choosing an apartment near the local train station.

In *Insel*, she comments that Oelze did not speak a word of French, and that his "will-o'-the-wisp" behavior extended to his association with the French Surrealists, with whose work his own paintings have been grouped and among whom he might have found kindred spirits, or at least sympathetic colleagues. But Oelze assumed the pose of the reticent mingler rather than the blind conformist in Breton's regimented inner circle, just as Loy had assumed the role of critical observer in her associations with the Italian Futurists and the New York Dadaists. Oelze hid behind the language barrier and the identity of the transient.

Along with a mutual respect for each other as artists, it may have been this shared aversion to wholehearted membership in groups that drew Loy and Oelze together. In all of her associations with the avant-garde—she was well-connected with the important artistic and literary circles of the first decades of the century in Europe and America before she became a virtual recluse in the Lower

East Side of New York—Loy fought to maintain her independence, and survival, as an artist. Likewise, Oelze seems to have developed a similar strategy with regard to the Surrealists. His first exposure to surrealist art came in 1921, when he saw reproductions of paintings by Max Ernst and Hans Arp in Ascona, Italy. The favorable impression they made on him eventually drew Oelze to Paris in 1933, where he soon met Ernst and struck up a friendship with Paul Eluard. He showed his paintings at a few of the Surrealists' exhibitions, but his contact with Breton's crew was sporadic at best, and when he did encounter them *en masse,* he acted coy.

As time passed, Oelze moved farther and farther from the group, preferring to shut himself up in his sparsely furnished workroom to paint rather than to be seen at surrealist events. Though concerned about his psychological well-being and the precise direction in which he was headed as an artist, Loy apparently respected Oelze for his fundamentally surrealist nature and his independence from the surrealist group. She seems to have believed that, in spite of his periods of inactivity, this behavior was evidence of a more serious dedication to his art. Throughout her life, she struggled with the conflict between an attraction to centers of artistic and literary activity—meeting the Futurists in 1913 had jolted her out of a long debilitating isolation—and the need to stay at home and work. In a 1929 *Little Review* questionnaire, she confessed that her greatest weakness was compassion, and her greatest strength was her "capacity for isolation."

The frequency with which social outcasts of every description appear in her poems and fiction reflects a concern about the possibility of maintaining one's integrity as an artist while part of a group, be it the middle class or the avant-garde. Her interest in Oelze continues this pattern of ambivalent feelings about avant-garde groups she had been associated with since she met Marinetti. Though she welcomed the heightened level of artistic activity and social life that surrounded avant-garde groups, she wasn't interested in collaboration; she couldn't abide by the tendency of the avant-garde to view works of art as means to political ends, for example; and there was no place for a serious woman artist in the elitist fraternities that these groups often became. Thus, it is not surprising that Loy was critical of the surrealist idea that the work of art is valuable only as a means of achieving the mental state of surreality, as well as of the Surrealists' tendency to view women as passive muses incapable of the work of the serious artist.

She takes her criticism of the Surrealists one step farther when she questions their very notion of what the surrealist state of mind actually is. Insel was, according to Loy, "more surrealistic than the Surrealists"; he "possessed some mental conjury enabling him to infuse an actual detail with the magical contrariness (that French) surrealism merely portrays." When Insel joked that the Surrealists wouldn't have anything to do with him because he'd ask them for money, Loy's narrator replies, "I should have thought you'd be *worth* a little money to a Surrealist. He might learn what supereality is about—you are organically surreal—. . . ."

In this way, Loy uses Insel to set herself not just apart from but far above the Surrealists while at the same time guarding against this quintessential Surrealist's instability and misogyny. The narrator's defiant farewell to Insel at the close of the novel sounds feminist but does not come across as hollow feminist dogma; her victory over his seductive aura and near violence is hard-won, and the tie to survival as an artist gives her victory more breadth. Loy's emphasis on preservation of the integral self or ego in *Insel* affirms her life-long concern about her identity as a practicing artist. In this sense, *Insel* can be read not only as an experiment in surrealist narrative, but as a satire on the whole surrealist endeavor. If this is true, the similarities between Loy's *Insel* and André Breton's *Nadja* bear more than a passing consideration. Loy may have actually structured her novel after Breton's in order to satirize him—as Victorian-styled middle class voyeur—and to express her indignation at the compromised role the Surrealists assigned to women.

Throughout her long career, Mina Loy kept a sober check on what glimpses of the other side the difficult and painful world can offer, partly because she recognized the futility of attempting to live in this world as if it were the next one, and partly because she was committed to producing an art with a measure of integrity. The limits Loy places on her narrator in *Insel* reflect this commitment, as does the narrator's victory at the end of the novel, when she asserts her authority over what up to this point has been for her a vision of overwhelming, and mostly destructive, power, with Insel in control. Finally, she is able to draw Insel's attention to *her* power. By transmuting his "*Sterben—man muss*" (Die, one must) to "*Man muss reif sein—*One must be ripe," she shocks Insel into a new way of seeing; he notices "*me* for the *first* time." The narrator has surpassed the richness in postponement that paralyzes Insel, and Mina Loy has completed her novel.

Elizabeth Arnold
Atlantic Beach, Florida

APPENDIX A
TRANSLATION OF FOREIGN WORDS AND PHRASES

t = top; m = middle; b = bottom

23 m *belote*   pinochle

25 m *Mädchen*   girl

26 b *Huissier*   sheriff (Loy's note)

28 m *Es war wirklich prachtvoll*   It was really splendid

34 b *Der Prozess*   The Trial

35 t *Zum Teufel*   What the devil!

40 b *Was haben Sie schönes erlebt*   What beautiful experiences have you had (Loy's note)

46 m *clochard*   tramp, hobo, bum

48 m *Elle n'a pas froid aux yeux*   She does not have cold eyes

49 t *Fleisch ohne Knochen*   boneless meat

55 t *carrefour*   intersection

57 t *Je suis la ruine féerique*   I am an enchanting ruin

58 b *La faim qui rode autour des palaces*   Starvation prowling palaces (Loy's note)

60 t I read later that sugar was used for strengthening concrete. (Loy's note)

69 t *Vielleicht verkaufen*   Perhaps to sell

70 m *Die nackte Seele*   The naked soul (Loy's note)

71 t *schade*   A pity (Loy's note), i.e., too bad!

73 t *Sterben*   To die

73 m *Sterben—man muss*   Die—one must

77 m *Unglaublich*   Incredible

78 t *consommation*   drink, snack

80 m *Ameise*   ant

83 m *cafés fines*   coffees and brandy

85 t *librairie*   bookshop

90 b *maquereau*   pimp

91 m *macrusallo*   (i.e., *maquereau* and *salaud* blended together)

93 m *plat anglais*   a plate of cold meats

98 b *Um Gottes Willen*   For God's sake!

100 t *Pfefferminztee*   peppermint tea

105 t *sommier*   divan

108 m *Strahlen*   rays

108 m *Ich bitte Sie*   I beg you

109 b *femme de ménage*   housekeeper

110 b *bidons*   cans

115 b *Der Totenkopf*   The death's-head (In earlier manuscript versions and in letters, Loy called the novel *Der Totenkopf.*—Ed.)

121 m *pour se faire une beauté*   to make himself up, to do his face

130 t *Chambres de Bonnes*   Maids' Rooms

130 b *Das ist die Irma*   That's Irma

133 b *Die Irma ist nass*   Die Irma is wet (Loy's note)

134 b *ou connait ça*   or knows that (obscure: perhaps a slip for *qui connait ça*, who knows that)

136 m *lustig*   jolly (Loy's note)

137 m *grand sympathique*   the sympathetic nerve

143 b *Gestatten Sie?*   May I?

146 m *Entwicklung*   development

147 m *écoliers*   school children

149 t *Sterben, man muss*   One must die (see p. 73)

149 t *Ich bin so müde*   I am so tired

153 b *Il dort dans son dos*   It sleeps on its back

156 t *Und Tatsächlich*   "And as a matter of fact"
        (Loy's note)

157 t *trompe d'oeil*   deceptive appearance, illusion

159 t The poet Arthur Cravan ("Colossus"), Loy's
        second husband, is considered a precursor of
        the Dadaists and a patron saint of the Sur-
        realists. (Ed.)

159 b *Seien wir uns wieder gut*   Let us like one
        another again, let's make up

161 m *die Rothaarige*   the redhead

174 b *um Himmels Willen!*   for Heaven's sake!

APPENDIX B
CHRONOLOGY OF MINA LOY

1882 b. December 27 "Mina Gertrude Lowy," London, England

1899 Studies art with Angelo Jank at Kunstlerrinen Verein, Munich

1901 Studies with Augustus John in London

1903 Moves to Paris; marries Stephen Haweis

1905 Enters Gertrude Stein's circle of artists and writers

1906 Elected member of Salon d'Automne; moves to Florence

1907 Joella Synara Haweis is born

1909 Giles (John Giles Stephen Musgrove) Haweis is born

1913 Meets F. T. Marinetti and other Futurist artists and writers; separates from Haweis

1914 First poems published (*Camera Work*)

1916 Sails for New York City where she enters Walter Conrad Arensberg's circle of artists and writers; meets Man Ray, Marcel Duchamp, Arthur Cravan, etc.

1918 Travels to Mexico; marries Cravan in Mexico City. She travels to Europe via Buenos Aires; he fails to meet her as planned; he is never seen again

1919 London; Lausanne; Florence
      Fabi (Jemima Fabienne) Cravan is born

1920	Returns to New York; deepens her ties with American avant-garde writers and artists
1921	Paris, Florence
1922	Florence, Vienna, Potsdam, Berlin
1923	Settles in Paris; first book of poems published (*Lunar Baedecker* (sic), Contact Pub. Co.)
1925	Narrative poem, *Anglo-Mongrels and the Rose*, completed
1927	Gives talk on Stein and reads her own poems at Natalie Barney's salon
1931	Becomes Paris representative for her son-in-law's (Julien Levy's) New York gallery
1933	Meets Richard Oelze
1936	Moves to New York; lives in the Bowery; friendship with Joseph Cornell; begins revising prose works begun in Paris, including *Insel*, presumably
1946	Becomes American citizen
1949	Moves to heart of Bowery; less and less contact with old friends living in New York
1953	Lives near her daughters in Aspen, Colorado
1959	Exhibition of her work, Bodley Gallery, New York
1966	Dies, September 25, in Aspen

(Adapted from *The Last Lunar Baedeker*, ed. Roger L. Conover (Highlands, N.C.: Jargon Society, 1982))

APPENDIX C
CHRONOLOGY OF RICHARD OELZE

1900	b. June 29, Magdeburg
1921-25	Studies at Bauhaus, Weimar; travels to Berlin, Hamburg, Leipzig, Köln, Düsseldorf
1926-29	Spends time in Dresden; more than a month-long visit at Dessau Bauhaus; travels to Essen
1929-30	Ascona
1930-32	Berlin; more than a month traveling in the Gardasee
1932	Late Fall: travels to Mainz and Frankfurt/Main
1933	March 31: takes train across the border to France; settles in Paris; loose contact with Breton, Dali, Eluard, Ernst; October: exhibits paintings in Salon des Indépendents
1936	October 1: leaves Paris for Switzerland
1936-37	Ascona
1937-38	Positano
1938	Returns to Germany: Essen, Mulheim/Ruhr, Magdeburg, Berlin
1939	Early in the year: settles in Worpswede
1940	Conscription and military service
1945	American imprisonment and release
1945-62	Worpswede

1951   Marries Hedwig Rohde
1953   Travels to Paris
1962   Moves to Porteholz bei Hameln
1964   Karl-Ernst-Osthaus-Preis der Stadt Hagen; other prizes
1965   Nomination as full member to Academy of Art, Berlin
1980   Dies, May 27, in Porteholz

(Adapted from *Richard Oelze 1900-1980: Gemalde und Zeichnungen*, hrsg. Wieland Schmied (Berlin: Akademie der Künste und Autoren, 1987), p. 185)

Printed November 1991 in Santa Barbara & Ann
Arbor for the Black Sparrow Press by Graham Mackintosh
& Edwards Brothers Inc. Text set in Lubalin Graph
by Words Worth. Design by Barbara Martin.
This edition is published in paper wrappers;
there are 250 hardcover trade copies;
& 176 numbered deluxe copies have been
handbound in boards by Earle Gray.

Photograph of Mina Loy by Man Ray, 1920. From the collection of Roger L. Conover.

ELIZABETH ARNOLD attended Oberlin College and wrote her Ph.D. thesis on Mina Loy for the University of Chicago's Department of English. After teaching and traveling in the American Northwest, she has settled in northeast Florida where she grew up. She now works as a legal secretary and free-lance copy editor while continuing to educate herself in the craft of writing poems.

ROGER L. CONOVER is Acquisition Editor for the Arts at the MIT Press and the editor of Mina Loy's collected poems, *The Last Lunar Baedeker*. He is currently preparing a new edition of Mina Loy's writings and a book on the lives of Arthur Cravan.